—Loveline

A CLASS ACT

LINDA HOLLAN

 PAN MACMILLAN

First published 1992 by Pan Macmillan Publishers Australia

This Lovelines edition published 1993 by
Pan Macmillan Children's Books
A division of Pan Macmillan Publishers Limited
Cavaye Place London SW10 9PG
and Basingstoke
Associated companies throughout the world

ISBN 0 330 33246 5

9 8 7 6 5 4 3 2 1

A CIP catalogue record for this book is available from
the British Library

This is a work of fiction. All characters and events in the story are
imaginary and any resemblance to any person living or dead is
purely coincidental.

Typeset by Trade Graphics
Printed by Cox & Wyman Ltd, Reading

Chapter 1

I sat in front of the mirror and stared at my own image. A girl with dark blonde hair and a round face looked back at me with just a touch of sympathy in her smile. Yeah, well we both knew what it was like to miss out on our futures, didn't we? I nodded at my reflection. And who wouldn't be extra miserable when two days after course offers went out, they didn't get a letter?

I grabbed my brush, pulled my hair back from my face and knotted it up, high onto my head. I liked the look of my face better that way. I gave myself a knowing look in the mirror and then couldn't help laughing. Funny the way you could do that — look so cool and confident in the bathroom mirror. I picked up a lipstick the colour of crushed berries, ran it over my lips, smacked them together and checked the corners of my mouth for smudges. 'Next ze eyeliner!' I said out loud. After some digging around in the make-up basket I shared with Mum I found it, and painted a wide black line, sixties style, over the top of my lids. I took a backward step and eyed myself carefully. Sure, my skin was far from perfect, and yes there where times when I would rather have looked like Julia Roberts than myself, eighteen year old Annie Jukova, but all things considered I figured I'd do for Australia's next great acting discovery. In fact, it wasn't all that difficult to imagine my face up on the billboards, playing lead in some incredible blockbuster. I'd be respected. I'd be admired for my talent. And my fans would adore me. Naturally, I'd give interviews to *TV Week* and *New Idea* but I wouldn't talk about things like children and husbands or secret weddings, no way! I'd have this super intelligent but warm and kind image, and when they wrote about me they'd say things like, 'We spoke to that honoured, loved and admired Australian Annie Jukova...'. I sighed and found my eyes in the mirror. The trouble was, it wasn't going to happen — not the way I'd planned it would, anyway. The truth was, I hadn't been offered a place in acting school and I didn't have a job. Come to think of it I didn't even have a boyfriend any more. Things were looking severely, radically, astronomically bad.

'Annie,' Mum's muffled voice called out through the bathroom door.

'What?'

'Can you come out here please?'

'No. I'm busy,' I lied. 'Go away.'

'We need to have a word before I go out.'

'Later.'

'Not later, now.' The bathroom door handle turned, but I'd locked it.

'Do you mind!' I called out. 'I don't go barging in when you're in the bathroom.'

'You've been in there for at least an hour, Annie. Be reasonable.'

'All right, all right. I'll be out in a minute.'

This had been happening a lot lately. Mum kept lurking around the house trying to corner me into these really depressing conversations about how I had to start being 'realistic.' God, I hated that word. 'Realistic' meant going down to the CES every day to look for a job and going into the city to enrol in a mindless course. I could just see it now, I'd be touch typing in ten days and then it'd only be a hop, skip and a jump into bed with some eligible doctor or lawyer and I could take acting classes after I'd dropped off our two point five children at school. I groaned out loud and caught my eye in the mirror. One more thought like that and the tears would be dripping down my face before Mum and I had even begun our little talk for the day. 'You're an actor, Annie,' I reminded myself. 'Get your act together.'

'Morning, Mum.' I smiled and headed for the kettle. 'How's tricks?'

'It's eleven-thirty.'

'Really?'

'Don't use that tone, Annie. It's not fair. I'm concerned about you. You don't go to bed until after midnight and then you don't get up until the day is half over. It's not good for you.' She snuck up behind me and put an arm over my shoulder. 'Your father and I have been talking and we'd like to make some clear rules about what we expect from you. That way you'll know where you stand and we won't have to constantly pester you.'

'And what about you?'

'Pardon?'

'Well, do I get to make up some rules for you and Dad?' I grabbed a mug out of the cupboard and slammed it down onto the bench.

'This is serious, Annie. I'm not about to let my daughter play games with me —'

'I don't want to play games with you.'

'You're living in my house. You're not bringing in any money and as a consequence, I think I'm in a position to tell you what to do.'

'And exactly what is it you want from me?'

'I've made an appointment for you with Talbot's Business College.'

A gigantic groan escaped me. 'I don't want to be a secretary...'

'But just listen to this.' Mum jumped up from her chair and reached for a glossy white folder lying near the phone. She cleared her throat and then began to read, ' "Talbot's offers courses designed for people wanting more than a secretarial position. Talbot's will train you in business management, advanced secretarial skills, personal assistance, and corporate ethics. We promise to equip you for a fascinating, rich and rewarding career — " '

'No! Thank you very much, Mum,' I said, carefully and distinctly. 'I appreciate your efforts to help me, but I'll die if you make me do this.'

'Don't be so melodramatic, Annie,' she sighed, 'you're not going to die while acquiring a few marketable skills.'

'I'm going to be an actor. Those aren't the sorts of skills I need.'

'I'm happy for you to pursue acting, but you're going to have to wait another year before you can apply again, and in that year — '

'I'm an actor now, school or no school. Don't make me do this.' I picked up the folder. 'You know it'll ruin my life.'

'Oh, Annie.' Mum dropped her head into her hands. 'What are we going to do with you? You can't just sit around the house all day. You have to be doing something.'

'I will.' I pressed my advantage. 'I'll ring up Josh today and we'll start working on his script. I don't know,' I raved on, 'maybe we can get some funding to make a small film and then I can use that when I apply next year. I've got a really good chance, you know. There aren't many kids who've already been in a film.'

'But that was several years ago.' Her eyes were sad. 'Yes it was wonderful that you got to go to Spain and be in a movie when you were fifteen but the fact is, you haven't done anything since then.'

'Because I've been at school but now's the time to change all that, which is why you just can't make me become a secretary.'

'All right.' Mum gave in. 'You've worn me down. You don't want to be a secretary? Fine, no one's going to make you become one. But you do have to work and if acting doesn't provide you with a job you'll have to find another career.

Annie, you're bright enough to do anything you want, even if it means going back to school to repeat or getting an apprenticeship.'

'Yes, yes, yes, Mum.' I waved it all aside. 'Let's not worry about that now. You go off to work and I'll see you later after Josh and I have had a chance to get things rolling.'

Josh and I were hot until pretty recently but we had this major problem in our relationship — we were both prima donnas. All the time I wanted him to pay me all the attention, he wanted someone to pay all the attention to him. We met at a school social — unbelievable but true. He was a poet at the time and I was an actor so it was pretty natural that we should seek each other out. Josh is kind of big with long, thick curly hair that he runs his fingers through all the time like he's got things on his mind. He wears a lot of black and talks about stuff like collective human destiny. Everyone used to think he was gay but he's not. He's just a performer. And he isn't all that serious either but you don't realise that until you get to know him. When we first started going out together we used to spend hours wandering around the streets at night, talking about the meaning of life, but after we got to know each other better we switched to eating and gossiping.

Josh and I went out together for a long time though. All through our last year of school and half of the year before that. Not that we were in class together, I was at a girls' school and he was at high school. Still, we managed to interfere in each other's work despite being in different places — we both ended up failing. Josh hit an all-time high in English and bombed out in everything else. I topped drama, passed English Literature, but didn't rate a mention in any other subject. No, that's not strictly true, my teachers wrote pages about me. Only trouble was, they weren't exactly complementary — which is probably why I dipped out on acting school.

'Josh, I need you.'

'I told you.' He sounded delighted. 'I said you wouldn't be able to last a week without me.'

'It's been two months.'

'A week, two months, what's the difference?'

'I need your script. I need your film. I never

said anything about your body or your person.' I lifted the phone from the kitchen bench and carried it over to the couch, realising this was going to be a long session. 'Listen, Mum's about to pay out on me so we need to move fast. I think I'd better direct, don't you? After all, I'm the only one with any experience.'

'It's my script,' he bristled, 'I'll direct.'

'Don't be stupid, Josh. I intend to use this to get work.'

'So do I.'

'Then you'd better let me direct. At least I've seen it done before. You're a writer, Josh, you know about words. I'm an actress. I know how to get things across visually.'

'I think we should co-direct,' he wheedled.

'That wouldn't work. We'd spend all day arguing about everything.'

Josh sighed. 'It's absolutely pointless. We're never going to make this film. We can't even agree about who's going to direct it.'

'Stop it, Josh. You know I can't stand it when you talk like that.'

'But it's true. We don't even have a camera.

And who are we going to use for actors? You might be a genius, Miss Smartypants, but you can't play three different people all in the same scene at the one time. We need to get some money together first and then —'

'I haven't got time for that. Mum's really pushing. So you agree I should direct?'

'Only because you bossed me into it, not because you're any better than I am.'

'Whatever you say,' I agreed. 'As for the camera, Izi can use Dad's video.'

'No way! I'm not ruining my film with video, it's proper film or nothing. Besides, my brother can't be trusted behind a camera.'

'Then it'll be nothing,' I pointed out, 'unless you know someone apart from Izi who has their own equipment.'

'I might.' He sounded smug. 'I know this woman called Rita. She's a camerawoman.'

'But would she do it for us?'

'Not for free.'

'Has she got her own equipment?'

'I don't know,' he admitted.

'This is hopeless.'

'I told you that already.'

'Now, Josh,' I picked up the phone and headed back to the kitchen bench, 'I want you to pay attention. We're going to make this film, and we're probably going to make it on video. And before you get on your high artistic horse just remember that you can use the video to get the money to make the film. Besides, if you don't get on with it you probably will need to "talk to someone" just like your mother keeps on telling you and everyone else who's prepared to listen.'

'Hey,' Josh brightened. 'Could you tell her we're still going out together?'

'No!'

'What sort of friend are you if you won't even tell lies for me?'

'She wouldn't believe me anyway.'

'It'd make her so happy and then she'd leave me alone for a while. Maybe I should get her to take up a hobby? Or suggest she goes overseas for a holiday?'

'See ya, Josh.' I waved my hand at the empty room. 'I'll be over at your house shortly to tell you what I think needs re-writing.'

'Now you're going to tell me how to write?' he snorted down the line.

'Half an hour,' I said firmly and put down the phone.

It took me a full twenty minutes to get enough money for the bus fare to Josh's house but at last I found the final twenty cents wedged under the leg of Dad's wobbly desk. I slipped it into the front pocket of my jeans and closed the front door behind me. On the way out I checked the mailbox — out of habit really, because I never got any interesting mail. There were four letters, a bank statement each for Mum and Dad, a card for Dad from my grandfather, and an overseas letter. I had to look twice before I realised it was addressed to me. I turned it over and saw that it was from Pascal in Spain. Pascal, my first boyfriend, the guy I'd been in the film with all those years ago! I hadn't had a letter from him for at least a year. I smiled as I walked to the bus stop.

Pascal had been like a dream come true for me. I remembered how hard it had been during those first few days in Spain, being in a different country, the youngest person in the film, with only my dad to talk to, but then I'd gotten to know Angela and her brother Pascal. And then I'd gotten to know Pascal even better. I laughed out loud and had to fan myself with Pascal's letter to chase the thought away. Well, now I'd have the chance to see what he was up to. My bus arrived and I had to put off opening the letter while I paid my fare and found a seat, but soon I was slipping my house key under the edge of the envelope and slitting it open.

Chapter 2

Dear Annie,

Surprised to hear from me, I suppose? I haven't been the best pen friend, have I? Well, you know how it is — school, home, social life ... Angela says 'hi' and wishes you were here. I don't even remember what I was doing the last time I wrote to you so I guess I'd better fill you in on the last year and a half. First of all, I'm not an actor any more. I've been in enough boring commercials to last me a lifetime. Really, Annie, acting is a dead end for anyone with half a brain. Have you come to the same conclusion? I bet you have. After I stopped acting I started paying attention to my studies so I got good marks in my final year at school. In fact, I got a place at university in Madrid. I study Spanish Literature. Are you at university too?

So, it's time to confess that I have a reason for writing to you apart from just wanting to let you know I haven't forgotten you. The truth is, I'm coming out to Australia and I want to know if I can stay with you. I would have written and asked you earlier but I only just found out myself that I'm taking this holiday. You see, I managed to buy the ticket for half price from this girl I know. She was taking a trip during uni holidays to visit her uncle and aunt but some family emergency forced her to change her mind. So I got her ticket.

Here comes the hard part... I'm arriving in ten days. I'd ring, except I've lost your number. Sorry about this. By the time you get this letter I'll probably be on my way. The thing is, if it's not all right for me to stay with you, you don't have to have me. I'm planning to do a bit of travelling around your country and I won't be any trouble. It would be good though, if I could sleep off the plane trip at your place. By the way, are you still as gorgeous as I remember? I suppose I shouldn't say

16

that to someone I hardly know any more.

Even if you can't have me to stay, I hope we'll still be able to spend some time together? I've got your address so I'll make my way there when I arrive on the twenty-eighth. I think I get in just before lunch. If no one is home I'll hang around for a while and then take off to a hotel or something. I really want to see you again.

Your old friend,
Pascal

I sucked in a deep breath of air and held on tight to the letter while I thought about what it said. I was all hot inside after reading that bit about me being gorgeous — finally, here was someone fatally attracted to me, fat face and all. But then again, what did I want with some Spanish lech breathing down my neck? What if I couldn't stand the sight of him? What if he thought it was still on, just because we'd gone out together all those years ago? Oh God! I groaned out loud at the thought, and then pretended I was coughing so the other passengers wouldn't think I had some sort of mental problem.

If the worst came to the worst, I could tell Pascal that Mum and Dad said he couldn't stay. Trouble was, they wouldn't back me up — especially Dad, he'd be falling all over himself to reminisce about the good old days, including his famous two minutes on film as an extra. I thought about the possibilities for a bit longer. Maybe I could say there wasn't much room at home and that I was really busy making this short film, so he'd be better off in a hotel? I chewed my fingernail absently and thought about it. I was being a coward.

The truth is, I have this habit of being a coward. Usually, I have it under control but whenever something comes up I'm not sure about, my cowardly side takes over and I'm thinking up all sorts of complicated reasons to get myself out of doing or saying things I don't want to do or say. Anyone else would be glad to see an old friend from overseas, but all I could think about was how nervous I'd be having an ex-boyfriend around the place. I wondered what he'd be like now and thought back to the first time I'd seen him. He'd had long black hair then, a thin angular face and smooth golden skin. And that's right, he'd worn these three silver stars in one ear. I'd been really blown away by it all at the time — talk about first impressions, talk about exotic! I hummed away to myself, picturing it all. Trouble was, I started to blush again and I had to give my face another quick fan with Pascal's letter.

I started to put the letter into my bag when it occurred to me to take another look at his arrival date. If he was arriving in a couple of days' time, I'd have a bit of work to do getting the spare room ready. I wondered if I should use Josh's phone to call Mum and Dad at work and let them know Pascal was about to descend on us.

'Excuse me,' I asked the woman sitting across from me. 'What's the date today?'

'Um, the twenty-eighth, I think. Yes, it's the twenty-eighth.'

'Are you sure?'

'Yes.' She smiled at me, kindly. 'Look, I'll show you in my dairy.'

She handed over a cloth-covered, pocket diary for me to examine. Sure enough, it was the twenty-eighth.

'I've got to get off the bus.'

'Are you all right, dear?'

'Could you let me off please?' I jumped up and stumbled towards the driver. 'I've got to get home, urgently.'

'You may as well stay on, love. This is the bus that'll be taking you back the way you came and there's only one more stop to the terminus. Unless you're thinking of catching a taxi, that is?'

'Ah... no,' I shook my head, remembering I hadn't any money.

'Well, sit back down and enjoy the ride.'

I sat back down but the last thing I did was enjoy the ride. The whole way home I had my bottom lip between my teeth and my right foot flat against the floor, pressing against an imaginary accelerator. Each red light was like a hot coal in my stomach and each stop along the way seemed to take a hundred years. What would Pascal think if he arrived and found no one at home? He'd think I wasn't much of a friend, that's what. Maybe I wasn't totally sure I'd enjoy having him to stay, but when it really came down to it I couldn't bear the thought of letting an old friend think I didn't care. God, how awful. My stomach started to burn again as I thought about what it would be like to arrive at Pascal's place in Spain and find it all locked up with no explanation about where anyone was.

A couple of stops from home I started to calm down and think things through again. The fact was, Pascal hadn't exactly given me much notice that he was coming. And... And come to think of it, it wasn't all that hard to get someone's phone number from international directory and give them a call, and ask them if it suited them to have a visitor come and stay. I couldn't be blamed for going about my own business when he hadn't taken the trouble to get hold of me earlier. I thought about him sitting on our front door step, wondering what to do, and couldn't stop a tiny smile creeping onto my face. Okay, so it wasn't all that nice of me to smile about Pascal having a hard time, but it wouldn't hurt his manners to suffer a bit. After all, I'd suffered plenty in the last twenty minutes.

By the time we reached my stop and I climbed

off the bus, I was feeling on top of the world again. I strolled down Lamont Street as though I had nothing on my mind except blue sky and sunshine. I'd planned to walk slowly all the way back to my place, but of course I ran the last bit — you have to admit having a mysterious guy land on your front door step has its exciting side. I pulled up before the front gate though, in case Pascal was watching, and luckily got a chance to check out the figure standing at my front door before he noticed me.

The years since I'd last seen him had given Pascal an extra ten centimeters or so and although he was still slight, his legs and arms were shaped by some pretty healthy looking muscle. He looked as though he'd been doing a bit of hard work. Come to think of it, he was dressed for it too. Last time I'd seen Pascal he'd been the last word in sophisticated European fashion, today he was dressed in a baggy old orange T-shirt and an ancient pair of shorts. If it wasn't for the way the light caught those three stars in his ear or the fact that I was expecting him, he could have been a complete stranger to me. At least that's what I thought until I got a closer look.

'Annie!' He opened his arms out wide and grabbed hold of me as soon as I got within arms' length. 'I thought I was going to have to sleep on your front step.'

'I only just got your letter.' I squeezed him back, and tried to ignore the feeling it gave me. 'Hey,' I laughed it off. 'You'd better come inside. You must be exhausted.'

When I feel nervous I talk a lot. I especially talk a lot with guys. It's that cowardly thing of mine again. I just can't stand silence unless I know someone really well. Put me in a room where no one's talking and I go into performance mode — full-on chatter. It's sort of okay when there's someone around to rescue me, but Pascal and I were on our own. I talked while I showed him the spare room. I kept it up all through showing him where the bathroom was and giving him a towel. I raved on about nothing while he sat at the table and I didn't draw breath until I sat down opposite him. We stared at the two mugs of coffee I'd made and I felt a blush slowly begin to creep up my chest and onto my neck. I'd completely run out of things to say.

Trouble was, I didn't know Pascal. I knew the Pascal I remembered from all those years ago, but for all I knew he probably had nothing to do with the Pascal sitting in front of me. I looked down at my coffee and then took a huge gulp to cover my embarrassment. The hot brown liquid bit at my tongue and a terrible choking sound leapt out through my nose as I tried to prevent myself from spitting coffee all over the table.

'Are you all right?'

'Umm.' I did my best to clear my throat. 'It went down the wrong way.'

Again the words dried up and I couldn't think of what to say. I'd already told Pascal about finishing school when we were in the bathroom. I'd even told him how great it was to have all that stuff over and done with — which wasn't even true because nothing terrified me more than having finished school. I'd talked about his trip while I was making him a coffee, and when we walked down the hall I'd told him how happy my parents would be to see him. All I was left with was the short film Josh and I were making and I already knew from his letter that he wasn't into acting any more! I don't think even that would have put me off except I wasn't sure how to make the film business sound interesting. After all, Josh and I hadn't actually done anything apart from argue about who was going to direct the thing. Then the telephone rang and saved me.

'I'll be back in a minute,' I said and whipped out the door.

It was Josh, wondering where I was and why it was taking me so long to get over to his place. I gave him the whole story, making it as long and drawn out as possible so I wouldn't get back into the kitchen too quickly. In the end Josh agreed to come straight over to rescue me by arriving with the script under his arm and then insisting that we spend the rest of the afternoon working on the finer points. Maybe Pascal would want to catch up on some of his lost sleep?

'That was Josh,' I explained on my way back into the kitchen.

I filled up another five minutes telling Pascal all

about Josh. Unfortunately I ran out of fascinating descriptions of Josh's amazing personality about twenty minutes before I could expect to hear his knock at the door.

'Another coffee?' I asked.

'No, I don't think so.'

'Something to eat?' I said, jumping up. 'You must be starving.'

'No, no.' He held up his hands, and gave me a wry smile. 'They do nothing but feed you on the plane. Really, I don't need anything.'

I sank back into the kitchen chair and looked around the room with what I desperately hoped was a relaxed expression on my face. I could feel his eyes on me but there was no way in the world that I was going to look in his direction. So long as he didn't catch my eye I could somehow pretend that everything was cool, that I was used to sitting around my kitchen table for hours on end with absolutely nothing to say to the person sitting opposite me. Every couple of minutes my blush would start to creep up my neck again and then I'd have to do this mental exercise of telling myself that everything was just fine and imagining myself swimming in a nice cool pool on a calm, relaxing sort of day. The first six times I tried it I tricked my body into behaving itself, but on my seventh attempt a wild thought about how idiotic the whole scene was, ruined everything and my face went bright red.

'Oh God,' I groaned, and put my hands up, covering my mouth and my cheeks. 'Don't look at me.'

Pascal stared at me intently.

'I said, "don't look at me". You're looking at me.'

'Sorry.' He did his best to stare at the top of the table. 'Did I do something to offend you?'

'No,' I snapped, forgetting I didn't know him well enough to snap at him. 'I blush easily. No, don't look,' I insisted as he started to raise his eyes. 'It's just this stupid thing that happens to me now and again when I don't know someone very well.'

'But you know me.' He looked up. 'We used to go out together.'

'That was years ago.' I waved a hand and accidently exposed one of my flaming cheeks.

'I don't remember you blushing. You were always quiet and maybe a bit shy but you didn't blush.'

'Well I do now.'

I grabbed a table mat and waved it in front of my face. There was no point in worrying about what I looked like now — Pascal had already seen enough.

'Don't be embarrassed.'

'Easy to say,' I pointed out.

'I guess so,' he agreed. 'Does it happen often?'

I made a face. 'Can we change the subject?'

'Sorry.'

He clammed up and there we were again, sitting at the kitchen table with nothing to say to each other.

I groaned again.

'What?' He looked up at me.

'It's the silences that do it. Can't you think of something to say?'

'Do you want me to go?'

'Of course not.'

'But I make you feel uncomfortable,' he pointed out.

'Just talk. Tell me something — anything.'

'Okay,' I could see him searching his mind. 'I've been going to university in Madrid…'

'I know that, silly, you told me in your letter.'

'Sorry, I'll try again.' He grinned at me. 'Here we go. My parents are well,' he sounded like he was rehearsing a prepared speech. 'They send you their love. Angela is engaged to a guy she's been out with for three years — '

'Engaged?' I burst in. 'How ridiculous! She's way too young.'

'That's not the way she sees it,' he pointed out.

'I bet it's not. Next thing you'll be telling me she's planning to have a couple of kids…'

'Four.'

'Four?' I raised an eyebrow.

'Four,' he repeated, solemnly.

At some stage — I suppose about fifteen minutes later — Josh arrived. Josh has a really big personality and he tends to take over if you let him. I never let him but there was a bit of a struggle when he first arrived because he thought he was coming over to rescue me from having nothing to say to my house guest, little knowing that once we'd gotten started, Pascal and I could hardly stop ourselves. Josh marched into the house, talking at the top of his voice about how fast we had to move on the script, how he knew I had someone staying but they'd have to understand how important our work was. Pascal was just sitting on the arm of the sofa, staring at Josh as though he'd never seen anything like him in his life before. I almost started laughing because it did look funny.

Like I said before, Josh is big with all this thick and long curly hair. When you know him properly you can see that it suits him, but in the beginning even I have to admit that he looks pretty strange — and I love him to death. And there he was in my sitting-room, stomping around raving on about how wildly important our work was together, looking like a complete idiot. In fact, he looked like a character actor in a thirties gangster movie. He was wearing a broad striped suit and he had one of those funny little black gangster hats perched on the back of his head. All that was missing was the violin case to hide his machinegun inside.

'Sit down, Josh,' I said, 'you're giving me a headache.'

'Sit down?' He spun on his heel and stared at me.

'Everything's fine,' I said, hurriedly. 'Just relax and maybe we actually will do some work this afternoon. You don't mind, do you?' I turned to Pascal.

'Fine with me. I can make myself scarce if you want me to.'

'No need. We love having you here, don't we, Josh?'

Josh wasn't all that keen but he wasn't game to say a word, so we all sat around the coffee table and began to talk shop. In the beginning it was mainly me and Josh talking but Pascal couldn't help himself and soon we were all raving away about the best way to shoot a particular scene or whether the dialogue was working smoothly enough. So much for Pascal not being into acting any more.

Chapter 3

'Give me the camera!' I shouted at Izi, Josh's kid brother. 'You're driving me crazy.'

'Josh said I could do what I want. "Complete artistic licence", if I remember his words correctly.' He backed away from me.

'Did he also tell you to leave your brain at home?'

'What's wrong with her today?' Izi turned his innocent blue eyes towards Josh.

'The woman is creating a work of art.' Josh grabbed his brother's ear. 'Listen very carefully to what she says and don't ask any questions. If we want your opinion we'll ask for it.'

'But it's such a dumb scene anyway.' Izi shook himself free, and made a face at his brother. 'Maybe a couple of pictures of you two arguing will add a little spice to the film. I mean, come on... You're asking us to believe that Annie — '

'Doreen,' I corrected him. 'My character's name is Doreen.'

'That Do-reen,' he stretched the name out, 'the uncrowned queen of netball has other interests?'

'Shut up and be quiet!' Josh shouted at Izi.

'Let him say it,' I said, icily. 'You never know, a miracle might happen, he might have a point.'

'As a matter of fact I do.' He sneered at me. 'The point is, if *The Great Netball Saga* is going to be a serious sort of farce, then it's got to go all the way. You can't have Doreen going off to rock concerts like an ordinary human being. The girl thinks, eats and breathes netball. Her scene is netball, and that's that. Rock is for other people, not for our Doreen.'

'Hey, that's not a bad idea you know,' Josh tapped the side of his nose. 'Eating a netball. We could have the whole family — Doreen, Colleen, Rayleen, Darleen, Aileen, and Herman — sitting down to a Sunday roast, only the roast is a netball. Get it?' He looked at me, excitedly. 'We'll have this enormous, great netball sitting in the middle of one of those Willow patterned plates, surrounded by roasted vegies, and dripping thick brown gravy. The picture's so real you can almost smell the aroma of the roasted leather and the spice of the gravy.' His nostrils flared. 'Herman carves it, slowly and precisely,' he made the motions with his hands, 'while Aileen and the girls drool over it. Then we could have them chewing it — and it's like leather! Man, it's tough. We can have them really ripping, snarling, chomping, and slurping all over the thing — gravy dribbling down their chins. Then we could flash direct to the ripping, snarling, chomping, and slurping of the netball court. Colleen is wing attack, Rayleen's wing defence, Darleen's goalie, and Doreen's centre — and they're going for it hammer and tongs. Aileen's screaming her girls on from the sidelines, coaching the hell out of them, and Herman's holding a plate full of oranges, cut into quarters. The oranges are for their glucose level at half time.'

'That is so stupid!' Izi sneered at Josh.

'It is a bit dumb,' I agreed. 'We don't want the script to degenerate into silliness, we want a proper comedy.'

'Well *I* think it's funny.' Josh's nose twitched the way it always did when he was angry. 'And I'd like to remind you that this is my script.' He patted his tattered copy. 'Essentially the writer is at the centre of the film — the writer owns the film. And you two,' he pointed at us, 'you have to trust that I know what I'm doing when I write a scene.'

'That doesn't mean we should all sit back and let you wreck it,' I pointed out. 'Let's just forget all this and get back to what we're doing. Izi,' I turned in his direction, 'you're a cameraman not a script consultant. Shoot the scene and talk about it later. Let's at least have a look at the results before we start fiddling with the story.'

'All right,' Izi grumbled, 'but I'm telling you it won't work.'

'And you, Josh,' I turned around to face him,

'get off Izi's back. Go and finish rewriting that last scene we shot.'

'If you don't mind,' Josh gave me a dirty look, 'I happen to have a part to play in this particular shoot — or had you forgotten?'

'Oh.' I did a double take. 'Okay then. I just forgot for a minute. Put your script down and lean up against the car over there,' I directed. 'Izi, I want you to go right down the end of the street and film me and Josh like we're just specks of dust on the streetscape...'

' "Specks of dust on the streetscape"?' Izi rolled his eyes. 'You're the boss.'

'And I'll walk toward both of you. Then I see Josh and run over to him and throw myself into his arms. And you, Izi,' I called after his departing back, 'you film straight down the middle. Don't emphasise either of us because we're just two people on the street...'

'Yeah, yeah, yeah,' Izi waved a hand. 'Specks of dust...'

'And then,' I turned to Josh, 'you and I embrace, kiss with closed lips and start walking arm in arm towards the concert hall. Ready, everyone?'

I put all thoughts of Izi, Josh and I out of my head and tried to think myself into the part. I waited about thirty seconds after Izi signalled and then started to walk down the road. Ten paces on I caught sight of Josh and broke into a run. He was leaning back against someone's old Commodore, with his hat tipped right back on his head. He didn't see me coming and took the full impact, as I threw myself against him. Josh put his arms around me and we kissed. For a minute it felt like old times again but we broke the embrace and began walking down the sidewalk in Izi's direction, Josh kicking at the leaves while I kept my eyes dead ahead.

Later that night, when we played the day's filming at my house, some of my certainty that I knew what I was doing began to slip away. For a start, everyone agreed that Izi had been right and the scene about the rock concert was totally out of place in the film — not only that, it was dead boring too. But it was the comedy scenes we'd shot that really brought things to a head. Doreen didn't look like Doreen at all — she looked like me worrying about whether everyone was doing what I'd told them to do.

'Hey, look at you there,' Izi hooted, and pointed at the screen. 'You're meant to be listening to Aileen coaching and you can't keep your eyes off what I'm doing with the camera.'

'And what about that?' I heard Pascal's low chuckle as he pointed to a shot of me going for a goal. 'I can see you sneaking a look at your watch.'

'I am not,' I snapped.

'Yes you are,' they all said, in unison.

'There,' Pascal jumped out of his seat and tapped the television screen, 'you're doing it again. You're looking at your watch to see how much time the scene's taking.'

'Well, everyone was fooling around,' I complained. 'Leela wasn't doing her part properly and Mum didn't look anything like Aileen is supposed to look, not to mention the fact that she had a meeting to get to at two-thirty and kept trying to leave all the time. Who wouldn't be looking at their watch?'

'Maybe we need to recast everyone?' Josh suggested.

'Go over all that again?' my voice began to catch in my throat. 'Josh, don't you remember what it was like trying to find enough people willing to help out for free? No way!'

'Face it, Annie, you've got too much to do,' Pascal said. 'Acting is a full time job, and you're trying to direct as well.'

'She's not only directing and acting,' Josh jumped in, 'she's also trying to boss me around by telling me what I can and can't do with my own script. It's just not practical, and it's not fair. I told you we should co-direct.' He turned to face me. 'Better still, let me direct. You're the lead, you can't expect to do everything. How about giving me a turn?'

'Or Pascal,' Izi suggested, always ready to stir the pot. 'Pascal's not acting and he's got more experience filming than you do, Josh.'

'Pascal's just a visitor.' Josh practically leapt out of his chair. 'Keep him out of it.'

'Stop it! Everyone just stop it,' I shouted. 'Josh, we've had this argument before,' I tried to keep my voice calm, 'and you know I've had more experience than you.'

'Well maybe you should get someone else to play Doreen?' Izi made himself more comfortable by resting his legs in my lap. 'Maybe you should concentrate on directing?'

'You'd be able to do a better job,' Pascal agreed. 'The film would get a more even look because you'd be able to watch from the outside, instead of one minute being in the thick of things as an actor and the next standing back and watching everyone else as a director. It'd make more sense.'

'I don't want to talk about it.' I pushed Izi's legs from my lap. 'I need some time on my own. I think you'd all better go home.'

'But we're filming again tomorrow.' Josh stood up and ejected the video from the machine. 'Let's not waste another day like we did today. Come on, Annie, you have to make up your mind either way. This isn't just about you. A lot of other people are putting time into this film and you can't just brush us off.'

'All right! All right, I give in.'

'Then you'll let me direct?' Josh could hardly keep the smile off his face.

'No,' I shook my head, 'someone else can play

Doreen. I want to see this film through. I know what it should look like. I know how the parts should be played and I think I'm the only one who can manage to get Mum, Leela, Dad, Mandy and Maria to play all those crazy parts properly — especially considering that none of them can act.'

'Great one, Einstein.' Josh looked nasty. 'And who's going to play Doreen? Face it, there isn't anyone else available except you. You're not that great a director that you can create an actor out of thin air.'

'You don't know how good I am.' I stared him down.

'I do so. Average for a beginner.'

'Oh yeah?' I challenged.

'Yeah. A really good director can make you believe anything.'

'Like what, for example?'

'That black is white,' Josh waved his arms about, 'that a papier-mache ball is a planet suspended in deep space, that a netball is a Sunday roast...'

'Easy,' I took the bait. 'I can do that. Maybe I'm

not crazy about the Sunday dinner scene, but I never said I couldn't shoot it.'

'You're on.' Josh sounded pleased.

'I've got a good one for you,' Izi's mouth curved into an evil grin. 'If you're as hot as you think you are, then you should be able to make us believe Pascal is Doreen. Let Pascal play Doreen.'

'Now that *is* stupid.' I gave him a withering look. 'Pascal's practically two meters tall, shaves once a day, and has legs that wouldn't look at all the part under a netball tunic.'

'Hang on a minute,' Josh sat forward onto the edge of his seat, 'that's not such a bad idea. Aileen and Herman have a son, okay? Only they can't cope with the disappointment of not getting another girl for the team so they name him Doreen and bring him up as a girl. Pascal dresses up in sandshoes and a tunic and plays his heart out. It's beautiful.'

I looked over at Pascal expecting to see an expression of horror on his face and instead I saw a huge smile.

'You wouldn't want to do it, would you, Pascal?' I asked, hopefully.

'I don't know.' He shrugged. 'I know it's crazy, but I kind of like the idea. And you do need someone to play Doreen.'

'Why don't we just cut Doreen out?' I suggested. 'Or cut Rayleen out, and Mandy can play Doreen instead of me?'

'Boring!' Izi groaned.

'But Pascal playing a girl? Come on.' I put my head in my hands. 'It's just too much.'

'What's it to be, guys?' Josh looked at Izi and Pascal, and they both nodded their agreement. 'Sorry,' he winked at me, 'looks like you're outnumbered. Still, at least you get what you really wanted — you get to direct.'

'Okay,' I sighed. 'Pascal it is.'

I took hold of one of Josh's hands and pulled him up out of the chair. 'You'd better take your brother and go home because believe me, I've had about enough of you for one day.'

'You're the greatest, Annie.' He smiled and put his arms around me. 'I know you're annoyed, but you won't regret this. This is going to be the funniest film we've ever made.'

'We've never made a film before.'

'See? I'm right already.'

The day had really taken it out of me, not to mention the evening. I hate it when everyone tries to get what they want and none of it fits in with what I want to do. Maybe I should have been happy that I still got to direct the film but another part of me kept wondering what was the point in directing something as completely ridiculous as our film was turning out to be?

When we'd originally started working on it — that day when Pascal first arrived — it had seemed like it really was going to be something special. Pascal, Josh and I had sat over the script and worked out all the funniest parts. Sure, Josh had the beginnings there in his original script but with the three of us sitting around, acting out the parts, heaps got added — and a fair bit got dumped too. When Mum and Dad came home we'd made them join in as Herman and Aileen — which is how I managed to persuade them to play those parts when we couldn't find anyone proper to do it for free. (They also said it was fine for Pascal to stay with us for a while.) And now? Now Pascal was going to be the main character dressed up as a girl. It wasn't that I couldn't cope with the pace of change, it was more a case of the whole project being hijacked by a pack of rampaging juveniles while I got stuck with directing the idiots.

I wandered into the kitchen, weighed down with the thought of the mess we were creating, and looked around me while I tried to figure out what to eat. I know, I know, eating for comfort is bad for you. But what do 'they' know about it, anyway? I made a savage grab at the box of Iron Man food and watched the pale brown, crunchy little treats tinkle into the breakfast bowl. I poured the milk in. The Nutrigrain swirled and spiralled around the spoon.

Pascal put his head around the corner of the kitchen doorway.

'Breakfast, Pascal? I like cereal when I'm worried.'

'Not for me, thanks. I won't ask you what you're worried about.'

'You don't need to,' I pointed out. 'You were in the thick of things.'

I picked up my bowl and followed him into

the sitting-room. Right in front of my eyes, he plonked himself down in my favourite spot. I stood there in front of him and willed him to move. I like sitting with my back up against one arm of the couch so I can watch television and keep an eye on the front window at the same time.

He looked around the room at all the empty chairs. 'Am I in your place?'

'Normally, I'd say no, but today I'll say yes. Move over. You can sit up the other end and talk to me. Just not about films, okay?'

'Deal.' He smiled and shifted further along the couch.

I put my legs up into the middle cushion, cradled my bowl of cereal, and made myself comfortable. 'Well, come on, then,' I waved a dripping spoon at him, 'talk to me'.

'Do you want to hear about university?'

'After not being accepted anywhere myself? You've got to be kidding.'

'Did you ring up that directing course in Melbourne?'

'Yeah,' I said.

'You don't sound very excited.'

'Well, what am I going to say to them? I've never directed anything — not even a school play. They want older people, who've had some experience. I haven't got a chance. I won't even get an interview, if you ask me.'

'No,' he agreed, 'I guess not.'

'Well, thanks a lot.' I gave him a dirty look.

'You're the one saying it. If you've already decided you're not the right sort of person for the course you certainly won't be able to persuade them to offer you a place.'

'Come on, Pascal, be realistic. I don't have any experience. They're not going to accept me.'

'Talk to them. Tell them about everything you've done. Tell them about our picture in Spain, about what you learnt from being in it and seeing it directed. Take along a copy…'

'I've already sent them one, so let's just wait and see.'

'Good! That's the way to do it. Then tell them about acting at school.'

'First I have to be invited down to see them. Besides, I hardly did any acting at school,' I confessed.

'Well, when they ask you down, tell them about what you did do — and why you weren't able to do more. Then finish off with anything you can think of about how you'd like to direct. After that, you can discuss whether you'd like to do films or plays and what sort of scripts you're interested in and why. Get right into it.'

'Why don't you go?' I laughed. 'They'd love you. They'd give you a place.'

'You've got to stop being so negative.'

'It's my personality. I'm shy. I'm pessimistic. It takes me ages to work out what I really think about things. Besides,' I looked at him, defiantly, 'I like being the way I am. At least it's honest. All that other stuff is so fake. It's just acting.'

'You're probably right,' he agreed. 'But maybe you just have to act the part if you want to get into the course.'

'Yuk.' I shivered.

'Are you cold? I'll get something to cover you.'

Pascal disappeared for a moment and came back with the big checked blanket from his bed. I put down my cereal bowl and Pascal draped the blanket over me. He climbed in at the other end and sat back in his spot.

'You can put your legs on my lap if you want to,' he suggested. 'You might be more comfortable.'

'Okay.'

I moved my feet over onto his thighs and rested them there. I hadn't touched Pascal apart from our first hello hug and I was a little uneasy about the whole idea but I thought I'd give it a try. We were old friends, after all. Without warning, I felt his hands close around my feet, holding firmly. I nearly flew off the couch.

'What are you doing?' I squealed.

'Nothing.' He pulled back, beginning to go a dull red around the ears. 'I was just going to move your feet and make them more comfortable,' he explained.

'Oh.'

'But you don't have to put them on my lap if you don't want to.' He looked embarrassed.

'But I wanted to.'

'Well, do then. I mean put them back on — if you'd still like to that is. Not that you have to just because you wanted to before. You might have changed your mind…'

I put my feet back onto his lap and waited. Nothing happened. He sat there as though he was made out of solid rock.

'Ah-hum,' I coughed. 'You can touch me. I won't jump this time.'

'No, no, no, it's okay.' He shook his head, quickly. 'I'm comfortable if you're comfortable.'

'Well, I'm not actually,' I confessed. 'I feel silly. Look, just put your hands back onto my feet and we'll pretend we've got exceptionally short memories.'

Pascal smiled and his whole body relaxed. A minute later I felt his warm hands touching my feet and somehow we just started talking again as though the way we'd both overreacted when we'd come into contact, hadn't meant anything. Well, probably it hadn't. What did I know about guys? Next to nothing, that's what. And what did I know about the vague feelings I'd been having about Pascal for the last week or so? Even less!

Chapter 4

'**A**ny special requests?' The man from Australian Airlines smiled at Pascal and I.

'We'd like a window seat, please,' I said. 'And I get it, Pascal, because you've been flying all over the place and I haven't done it for years.'

'Twenty-six A and B.' The man handed back our tickets. 'Enjoy your flight. Next please.' He looked over our shoulders.

'Let's take a seat,' Pascal suggested. 'We should be boarding soon.'

We sat down in two incredibly uncomfortable

plastic chairs that overlooked the side of our plane. I leant back, resting my feet up against the wooden rail protecting the picture window and Pascal did the same. Beside us sat two packs — Pascal's covered in old baggage stubs, mine clean and new with all my best interview clothes inside. To my complete amazement, I'd been asked down to Melbourne for an interview about the directing course, and Pascal had decided to come along with me as a tourist. It must have been the copy of the movie in Spain that got me in. I'd written a letter with all this stuff in it about how great I was, but lots of people would have done that.

'Hey,' I turned to Pascal, 'do you think they ask everyone to come in for an interview, or just a couple of people?'

'Didn't you check?'

'No.' I shook my head. 'Are you kidding?'

'What's so strange about asking? That would have been the first thing I'd have done.'

'I didn't want them to think I was pushy. They mightn't have liked it. And I want them to like me. Hey, I need them to like me!'

52

'You're meant to be pushy if you direct. And you are too.' He smiled at me.

'I am not!'

'You are so. It's just that you don't do it with strangers. When I first arrived, you weren't at all pushy.'

'No, of course not,' I agreed.

'But then,' he held up his finger, 'after we started to get to know each other better, and after I started helping with the film, you were ordering me around, the way you do Josh and Izi.'

'That's only because I had to. I'm not like that usually. Besides, it's not Josh and Izi, it's Mum, Dad, Leela, Maria and Mandy too. I have a whole cast I have to work with. You make it sound like it's only with the guys that I'm like that, and that's not true. I treat everyone the same.'

'So you admit it?'

'What?'

'That you're bossy.'

'*No.*' I had to laugh at the way he'd caught me out. 'Only when I'm working. Come on.' I stood up. 'Let's get on the plane.'

We shouldered our packs and followed the

queue into the plane's fat belly. They locked us in and then the flight attendants went through their safety routine as we taxied down the runway and prepared for take-off. We halted for a moment and then, as I looked out the window and watched the scenery slip by until it was just a blur, we rose up into the air like an awkward pelican carrying too heavy a load. Once we were up it was different. You couldn't even notice the engines running or the speed at which we were travelling. I relaxed back into my seat and slipped my shoes off.

It felt good being in the airplane next to Pascal. We could have been anyone up there in the sky. Two lovers jetting off across the world. Two smugglers heading across the border. Two strangers who'd spend a few hours together and then never meet again in their whole lives. Of course I wasn't going to tell Pascal all of that stuff, but that's how it felt. It was sort of like being completely free and completely separate from the rest of the world down below — including parents and studies and work, and the hassles that went along with all of that. I shook my head

and ran my hands through my hair. No, I wasn't
going to spend my first solo holiday thinking
about parents et cetera. All of my holidays to date
had involved adults or family tagging along, and
believe me, those sort of holidays had warts on
them.

I looked over at Pascal. He was stretched out
in his seat, his legs disappearing under the seat
in front and his head resting back against the
cushion behind. He held a book in his hands
but I could tell he wasn't really reading. His lids
dipped too low and his breathing went too deep.
That suited me just fine. Pascal had been at my
place for around two weeks and I hadn't had
a chance to really get a good look at him. You
can't exactly examine your guests at close range
without totally making a fool of yourself. You
especially can't do it when your guest is this guy
you almost don't know but you used to go out
with once upon a time.

It would have been different if Pascal were
a girl. If he were a girl we would have
been hanging out in the bathroom putting on
make-up, or at the very least squeezing a few

pimples, and we would have seen each other up close. It's like that with girls. I know what all my friends look like — in total and complete detail. Mandy has nice freckles the colour of dark chocolate. From a distance her face looks muddy with them, but closer in you can see how sweet they are. She looks as though she's been dusted with all these tiny, weeny patches of soft black skin. And Leela? Leela's got one of these really hairy faces. Not that she has a beard or anything. Her face is covered with peach skin fur — blonde and soft. You can't even see it unless you are quite close. Well, not exactly that close. I mean you don't need a microscope or anything! You can see it sitting next to her in class.

Pascal stirred and I looked over in his direction. His skin was thicker — guy's skin. Not that it was awful or anything but it was definitely thicker than a girl's would have been. His face was mainly smooth and didn't need much shaving, but around his chin and his upper lip, you could see darker patches. Not that Pascal let the hair grow or anything revolting like that. There's nothing worse than guys who let it grow when they haven't really got enough for a proper beard. I looked at his wide cheekbones and then at his eyes, where his skin thinned out to be almost translucent. It looked nice. He didn't have a perfect face, but it was kind and there were tiny wrinkles around his eyes from where he smiled. He smiled a lot. Not that I was interested, but I didn't mind looking out of pure curiosity, and with the best of possible motives. A small sigh escaped me as I examined the outline of his face for the second time.

He opened an eye. 'What are you looking at?'

The blood shot directly to my head. 'Nothing. Ah… Nothing. Really.' I laughed. 'I just glanced in your direction and then you woke up. Fancy that.'

'You were staring at me. I could feel your eyes on me.'

'I wasn't.' I shook my head. 'I was just… I was just seeing if you looked … If you looked much older,' I said, in a rush.

'Much older?'

'Older than the last time I saw you.' I waved my hands about a bit. 'You know, it's been years

57

and you could've changed a lot. In the face, I mean. People do. Change, that is.'

'Do you need to look so closely to tell?'

'No. I mean yes. You have to look but it's not staring or anything. It's just that I looked at you and then I started to think of something else and then I forget I was looking at you and then you jumped up and accused me of looking at you.'

'But you weren't?'

'No, not at all.' I shook my head, vigorously. 'I was thinking.'

'You're really weird sometimes.' He smiled at me.

'Don't be silly.'

'No,' he insisted. 'You are. But nice. Nice weird.'

'You just don't understand me,' I said. 'I'm the most ordinary person in the world. I'm so ordinary I can't stand it sometimes.'

'You see? That's weird.'

'No it's not. It's just that I'm honest. I spend all this time worrying about everything; worrying about what people think of me, about what people say about me, about what they might say if they knew what I thought, about what they might say if they just went ahead and said what they were thinking anyway without worrying about what I'd think if they did. I even worry about worrying. Mind you, everyone does that, it's just that they don't tell anyone because they want to have this image. Worrying isn't exactly the greatest thing for your image.'

'No, but...'

'So that's why people pretend they're so relaxed about everything. Me, I'm not relaxed and I'm not ashamed to admit it.'

'But some people are relaxed,' Pascal said.

'They're not really.' I folded my legs up underneath me, and made myself more comfortable. 'Those are just the sort of people I'm talking about — the ones who don't want to admit that they worry.'

'I don't worry. I'm relaxed.' Pascal spread his hands.

'I find that hard to believe.' I narrowed my eyes and looked at him carefully.

'I am. I just don't worry about anything. I don't care what people think about me.'

'Then you must be the weird one, not me, because that's unnatural.'

Pascal laughed. 'You're nice.'

'Don't say that.'

'Why not?' he asked.

'You just don't say things like that.' I felt my neck begin to burn. 'What am I supposed to say in return?'

'That's up to you.'

'Then I won't say anything.'

'Okay.' He smiled. 'But you are nice.'

And I didn't say anything. I just picked up my book and put my face in it. Sometimes Pascal came out with this stuff that you just couldn't do anything with. Apart from ignore it, that is — which is what I did. Anyway, he didn't carry on after that. He just went back to sleep until the plane landed and bumped him awake again.

Dad had organised our venue with some ancient crony of his. My parents had always been pretty strict about what I was and wasn't allowed to do, but as soon as I'd received the letter asking me to come in and talk about the directing course with an interview panel, the pair of them were off and racing. It was Mum who suggested Pascal go with me and Dad who rang up this friend of his to find us somewhere to stay. Pascal and I originally wanted to stay at a backpackers' hotel but in the end we decided to stay at the friend's house. We weren't crazy about the idea but I needed to be somewhere where I'd be able to get ready for my interview — and my folks absolutely promised that they weren't sending us into anything horrible.

We caught a tram from the centre of Melbourne into St Kilda, and then walked through the back streets until we found Dad's friend's house. She was home, which was good. She seemed kind of nice, which was amazing considering. And she only had time to show us to our rooms before she had to leave on a date, which was a bonus because I don't like sitting around talking to old people I hardly know.

I had an upstairs room right under the roof, with a little window looking out over the bay. The late afternoon sunshine streamed in onto my bed, giving the room a golden red glow. I dumped my pack and lay back on the faded cotton bedspread with my eyes closed. It was nice. I could feel heat underneath me from where the sun had warmed the cover, and a warm band across my chest from the light through the window. I decided to rest just for a minute before changing out of my travelling clothes. At first I thought about ordinary stuff, like Josh and the interview ahead of me. Then, as my head roamed around a little, I got back onto the subject of Pascal.

Our romance had been a short one. We'd only gone out together for the last few weeks of filming and then I'd had to return to Australia. I wondered whether it was my fate to have history repeat itself, only this time with Pascal in my country? Not that I believed in rubbish like fate but like I said, my mind was wandering all over the place. And it was true that I felt something for him. I certainly wasn't in love with Pascal. I liked him. He was nice. Really nice, only I didn't love him. You have to know someone to love them. I loved Josh. Just the thought of Josh made me feel all soft — but not the right sort of soft to go out with. Not any more, anyway.

With Josh, soft was feeling kind and sweet. With Pascal, soft was feeling... Well, it was feeling... It was feeling those things too but... I sighed and tried to mentally clear my head. The point was, I had to admit to myself that I was absolutely and completely attracted to Pascal. One look at his body and I was gone — or more precisely, my body was gone. I waved a hand over my face, feeling the beginnings of a blush. After a couple of minutes I let it fall back to my side and took up my train of thought again.

Before Pascal and I started going out together that first time, I'd been absolutely frantic — wondering about whether he liked me, how much he liked me, and what it all meant anyway. I'd never been out with anyone in my whole life before that, so I had no idea about all the signs to look for. Even worse still, once we started going out together I got totally freaked out by the whole thing. The first time we kissed I spent the whole moment wondering how to get out of it if I changed my mind. Then, when I decided I didn't want to change my mind, I spent the next few days worrying about whether Pascal would want to sleep with me and how I'd go about saying no to him without him thinking I didn't like him. I went round and round in circles until I didn't know what I thought about anything. It had seemed really complicated at the time, but I was much younger then. I laughed. Not that sorting things out with guys was easy once you get older.

Sex was still something I found impossible to work out. And it wasn't even that I'd had a whole lot of practice talking to guys about it because I hadn't had that many boyfriends, but I'd had to sort it out a couple of times. The most recent time was with Josh and before that with two other guys I'd seen for a while. It was cool with Josh, of course. Josh and I were friends, and if you're friends than you can talk about it without getting so embarrassed you feel like throwing up on the spot. I just told Josh I wasn't ready to do it and that I'd have to drop him if he ever hassled me about it. He was fine. One of the other guys hadn't been that simple though. He'd been full of that stuff about how he couldn't do without it for a single second longer because he was in

agony and how everyone did it so I should too —
and on, and on and on. Boring! Needless to say,
we lasted about two months. Later on he got this
other girl pregnant because he wouldn't wear a
condom. Some guys... A shudder ran through
me at the thought. I couldn't believe I'd ever
gotten involved with him.

If you say no to guys about sex it's as though
you don't want to do it at all, as though you're not
having to say no to yourself at the same time as
you're saying no to them. I really hate that. Most
of the times I've said no there's been a part of me
that really wanted to do it — even for curiosity's
sake. I used to have this idea about finding
someone to do it with who'd just disappear
afterwards so I wouldn't have to see him again
if I didn't like it — or if I regretted it. Sometimes I
wished I *had* done it with Josh because at least we
could've kept on being friends afterwards. At the
time, when I'd decided not to, it was because I
wasn't in love with him and I thought I had to be
if I was going to do it. Really though, he would
have been a good person to try it with for the
first time. I sighed, then sat up on the bed and

looked at the darkening sky and the silver and black water spread out in front of the sinking sun. I pulled some clothes out of my pack and began to dress.

Funny that I was thinking about sex all the time. I thought about sex a bit, of course — well, quite a lot actually — but I'd been thinking about it all that day, and that wasn't like me. I wondered whether Pascal thought about it too. He would of course, because everyone did. But what I was really curious about was whether he thought about having sex *with me*. That was the crucial point. Oh God. I sighed again and pulled on my jeans. There really was something going on between us and I hated to think how complicated that was going to make things. I had a film to make, a course to get into. I had a cast to manage and an ex-boyfriend who still carried on as if he adored me. Let's not forget the fact that I also had my parents watching over me — and they knew that Pascal and I had a history together. I groaned and buttoned up my shirt.

How could Pascal and I have a relationship anyway? I flopped back down on the bed. He was going back to Spain and I was staying put. He was going to university in Madrid and if I was moving anywhere at all, it would be to Melbourne. No, the best thing would be to ignore my feelings and keep things on a strictly friendship basis. There was no point starting anything when I had so much to do and he only had a few more weeks in the country.

I felt better after that. I brushed my hair, put on some eyeliner, and checked myself out in the mirror. The trick was to keep romance out of my mind and get on with more important things, like my career in film. Pascal and I obviously weren't meant to be — not this time anyway.

Chapter 5

'**W**hy directing, Annie?' asked a woman in a green woollen suit.

I glanced at her and then the three other people interviewing me while I searched for a good answer. It wasn't easy thinking on the spot, trying to find the right approach to take while they breathed down my neck.

'I guess because it seems more interesting to me than acting,' I said.

'In what way?' the old guy sitting next to her asked.

'Well,' I searched my mind, desperately, 'acting

seems really exciting before you've done much of it — and I guess in a way it is — but the really exciting part of any performance is the...' I lost track of my sentence completely and felt the heat start to creep up my neck. 'Well, it's the... Sorry, I'm a bit nervous.'

They stared at me and waited.

'Right.' I cleared my throat and willed my blush to die down. 'I suppose that what I'm trying to say is that when you direct, you put it all together. You make the story come to life in whatever way your mind's eye sees it.'

'But since you haven't tried it, it could turn out to be like acting was for you?' The woman in green raised an eyebrow. 'Glamorous on the outside but...' She cocked her head to one side and waited.

'I'm sorry?' I stared at her, blankly.

She sighed. 'You might well find it's not nearly as exciting as it looks.'

'Yes... I mean no.' I shook my head. 'It could be like that for some people but not for me. I'm directing a short film at the moment and it's great. It's fabulous. It's what I want to do.'

'Did you bring anything with you?' asked a woman with bright orange and purple hair.

'On film?' I asked.

'Any of your rushes. We're interested in seeing anything you've directed, even if it's unedited stuff.'

'I didn't think...' I tailed off.

They shifted in their seats and seemed to glance at each other out of the corners of their eyes. I decided to go on the offensive.

'To be honest I did briefly consider bringing something with me,' I lied, 'but I decided it wouldn't be a good idea. Not yet anyway. I'm not scared about letting anyone see what I've done but I do want to give myself a fair chance, and showing you the first two days' filming wouldn't be giving myself a fair chance. I'd like to at least find my feet and then I'd be happy to send some rushes down. Perhaps I could get something to you by the end of next week?'

'Yes, thank you.' The old guy relaxed a little and rocked back in his chair.

'So why do you think we should give you a place in our course?' A youngish guy, in a St Kilda

Arts Festival T-shirt, leant forward and glared at me.

'I can't really give you any fantastic reason. I guess I know I want to do the course — that I'll get a lot out of it — but I can't prove it to you.'

'Well, you'll have a chance to do just that tomorrow when you work with some of our first year actors,' he said.

'Oh, I didn't mean that,' I said. 'I mean, I know we're all doing that tomorrow — with the directing workshops and everything. I just meant that I can't really show you how serious I am about directing. I can say it, but I can't prove it.'

'So you think mental attitude is important?' the woman in green asked.

'Yes.'

'Can you tell us something about that?' The old guy looked at me as though he'd just asked me an absolutely fascinating question.

I smiled a little. 'You can have all the talent in the world and never do anything if you're not serious about what you want.'

'And you know what you want, do you?' the coloured haired woman asked.

'A bit.' I shrugged.

'You don't seem very sure.' She narrowed her eyes.

'This is only my fifth month out of school. I think I'm sure about what I want but I'd be lying if I said I had a completely closed mind about it.'

'What other courses have you applied for?' the woman in green asked, quickly.

'Acting.'

'I thought you didn't want to act,' she pointed out.

'I'd rather act than do something unrelated to drama, and there aren't that many directing courses around.'

'Yes,' she agreed. 'That's something we all regret. You're not a Melbourne girl, are you?'

'No. This is my first visit here.'

'And if you get into our course?' she continued. 'What then?'

'I'll move here.'

'Do you live at home now?' she asked.

'Yes, but mainly for financial reasons.'

'You might think that this is none of our business.' The guy in the T-shirt gave me a kind look. 'But we know from experience that there's no point having someone in the course who can't handle the stress — and there's a great deal of stress involved. Our students often work six days a week. When we're organising a performance they work seven days a week, and evenings too. You might have to be in class all day and then come back for rehearsals at night, not to mention keeping up with your general academic assignments. If you're not handling being away from home, you're not going to be able to cope with all of that.'

'I'll be fine.'

'How do you know?' asked the coloured haired woman.

'I just know.'

She glanced at the woman in green and I realised I'd made a mistake with that last answer.

'Look,' I smiled at her, trying to make her warm to me, 'I've travelled, I've worked a heavy schedule before, and I've coped. Admittedly, I had my dad with me but I was only sixteen at the time. I'm a lot older now and I can't see any reason why I wouldn't be able to cope just as well as the other students. Maybe even better.'

'Well, you certainly seem keen.' The old guy stood up and closed his notebook. 'I'm looking forward to seeing what you'll do with our little piece of theatre tomorrow. You know where to come to?'

I stood up and slung my bag over my shoulder. 'The back door of the theatre, and knock loudly.'

'We'll see you then.' He held out his hand for me to shake.

I rang Mum and Dad as soon as I got back to the house. Pascal made me a cup of tea as I sat up at the kitchen bar and talked into the phone until my ear began to ache. I had to give each of them a blow-by-blow description of the interview. I had to organise with Dad for the next week's filming. I had to persuade Mum to take a week off work to give the part of Aileen her full attention. On my way home I'd worked out exactly what I was going to do. I wanted to send the finished film down to the selection board, so I had to organise everything in a hurry.

Next I rang Josh to tell him about the interview and he was great. He promised to force Izi to give up his week to help us and to start searching for the right location for the scenes we needed to shoot. You can always count on Josh. He's the sort of guy who doesn't let you down even if there's nothing in it for him.

'And how's Melbourne?' he asked, after we'd settled all of the business.

'I don't really know. I haven't had a chance to look around.'

'I would've thought you and Pascal would have hit the town by now.' His voice tightened just a fraction.

'I haven't had time,' I explained. 'Pascal's been cruising around on his own and I'm sure he'll know this city better than I do by the time we get back.' I smiled at Pascal and he winked back at me.

'But you'll be out tonight?' he pressed.

'Jo-sh.' I rolled my eyes, even though he couldn't see me. 'Just don't, okay?'

'Don't what?'

'You know,' I said, not wanting to say anything more with Pascal listening.

'I can't help being jealous,' he whispered,

warming to the subject. 'It's not my fault if I'm passionately in love with you, if the sight of you turns me to jelly, if a glance in my direction can make me or break me. Annie, admit it, our destinies are intertwined.'

'Come off it, Josh.' I laughed.

'They are.' He sounded offended. 'You don't know how I feel. There you are with Pascal hanging around you. I mean, anyone can see he's crazy about you too but just remember he's not linked to you the way I am. You're not soulmates and it'll never work out between you.'

'And how would you know?' I rolled my eyes again.

'A guy can tell.'

'Don't give me that,' I snorted. 'Look, Josh, we're not having this conversation. You're embarrassing yourself and you'll regret it later.'

'I have no regrets! All I have is my passionate heart.'

'I'll speak to you tomorrow,' I ignored him. 'I've got to prepare for the theatre workshop now, so I'll have to hang up.'

'That's right,' he sighed. 'Cut me off just like

that. Now you've got Pascal to talk to you're not interested in talking to me...'

I hung up the phone. I do that sometimes with Josh. It's the best way to handle his temperament. He can get himself really worked up, but it's more the drama he's into than anything else. Like him saying he was passionately in love with me — it wasn't true and we both knew it. We were more like brother and sister than anything else. The problem was he was missing having a girlfriend so he thought it was worth persuading me to give us another try.

'What was that all about?' Pascal asked.

'Oh nothing.'

I climbed off the bar stool, walked around into the kitchen, and got busy buttering pieces of toast. There was no way I was going to tell Pascal about Josh. Not just because it would have been embarrassing for me — just imagine it — there was my loyalty to consider as well. Telling Pascal about Josh would be letting Josh down in a pretty nasty way. Anyway, Pascal didn't press it. He must have sensed that he was treading on private territory because he went out of his way not to mention Josh for the rest of the evening and to be extra polite and nice to me. Not that we had much time for intimate stuff anyway — I had the script the interview panel had given me to work on.

A couple of times that night I had to stop and pinch myself. It was hard to believe that I'd managed to get myself into a situation where I was going to have three hours to prepare five actors I'd never met before, to present my scene in a way that would convince the panel I had some sort of visionary potential as a director! Even the thought of it made me groan. I was either amazingly brave or a complete idiot. I didn't dwell on the fact that I'd never been known for my bravery and therefore was probably a complete idiot, but my stomach kept turning over and reminding me of the possibility.

At about ten-thirty Pascal suggested we leave directing alone for the night. We'd talked the script inside out. We'd thought up all these different ways of interpreting it. We'd discussed where the actors should stand on the stage and which props should be used. There was nothing more we could do. There was nothing more I could do. I needed sleep. My head ached from the rush of travel from the day before, the interview that afternoon, and all the thought we'd put into the evening. Walking up the stairs, I could feel all the muscles in my legs and my back tightening up and pulling at me. Pascal watched me climb.

'Are you going to sleep now?' I stopped for a minute, leant on the banister, and looked down at him.

'I don't think so,' he said. 'I'm full of energy.'

'Maybe you should go out? This isn't much fun for you.'

'I can go sight-seeing any time,' he pointed out.

'Sorry about this.' I waved my hands around, and then dropped them by my sides.

He shifted about, awkwardly.

'Is there something wrong? Because really, you can go out if you want to. I wouldn't mind at all.'

'No, no. It's not that. I don't want to go out. I'd hate to go out.'

'What is it then?'

'I, ah...' he broke off, looking uncomfortable.

'What?'

'No, it doesn't matter.' He shrugged.

'Tell me.' I leant further over the banister and looked down at him.

'It'll sound stupid. You might take it the wrong way.'

'Say it! You won't know unless you give me a try.'

'I was just wondering if you wanted someone to rub your back? But not like, you know...' he paused. 'Not like anything, or anything. Just your back, if it's sore that is.'

He looked down at the ground and scuffed his toe about a bit.

'Rub my back?' I repeated.

'Yeah.' He shrugged again. 'You said you were tired. It might help you sleep — relax you or something.'

'Thanks.'

'Does that mean yes or no?' He looked up at me, waiting.

'Well, yes. If you're sure you don't mind. Shall I come down or do you want to come up?'

'I'll come up. If that's okay with you, that is?

You do want to get to sleep after all. Unless you don't want to in your room? Have a massage, I mean. You might not want to?' He looked at me, appealingly.

'In my room is fine. Come on up.'

Pascal followed me into my bedroom. A part of me was all over the place, having him so near me and knowing I was about to come as close as I was probably ever going to get to feeling him next to my skin. The other part of me was just as preoccupied with the script as I had been earlier in the evening. I doubted I'd be able to sleep. Then again, I doubted I'd be able to sleep if Pascal didn't give me his massage.

'So?' I smiled at him, sheepishly. 'What am I supposed to do?'

'Lie face down on your bed. Have you got any sort of oil I could use?'

'Hardly.' I shook my head.

'It doesn't matter.'

I sat down on the edge of my bed and took off my shoes. Pascal looked at me and waited. We stayed like that for a minute or two and his face broke into a wide grin.

'I can't massage your back while you've got all your clothes on,' he said.

'Well, I'm not taking them off!'

'Not all of them,' he agreed quickly, going a bit red.

'I could take off my shirt, I guess, but you'll have to turn around.'

Pascal turned around and I slipped off my shirt and bra. I pushed them out of sight, under the bed, and lay down on my stomach. After I felt settled I told him I was ready. He sat down on the edge of the bed and rubbed his hands on his jeans to warm them up. He sort of chatted to me while he worked on my back and I listened with only half an ear, the other part of me drifting along with the feel of his hands. There was nothing sexual about it. Well, that wasn't strictly true — the feelings were there, but I knew nothing would happen unless I made it happen. I wasn't going to make it happen and Pascal certainly wasn't making any moves.

He worked on my shoulders first, digging his fingers into the muscles and running his thumbs over my shoulderblades. Every so often, he moved his hands up and pressed the tips of his fingers into the back of my neck and the base of my skull, moving them in circles, loosening up all the knots of tension and worry. I couldn't help the sighs escaping me, but somehow I didn't feel embarrassed about it. Slowly, he moved further down my back, concentrating on the length of my spine. He ran his hands along each side of my backbone until he got down to the top of my jeans, then he worked his way up again rubbing the flat of his palms over the entire area. It was soothing and warm, but I still wasn't going to be able to sleep.

'Are your hands getting tired?'

'No, I'm fine. How about you?' he asked. 'Are you falling asleep?'

'No.' I smiled, even though he couldn't see it. 'I feel good. My muscles have stopped aching but I can't drift off. I can't switch off my brain. All I can think about is tomorrow and what I'm going to do. Look, if you want to stop just stop.'

'No, I'll keep going.'

He kept working my back for about another twenty minutes. Neither of us spoke. I sighed now and again and Pascal grunted occasionally with the effort of kneading my skin, but apart from that the whole house was still. My body went deeper and deeper into itself, letting go of everything, but still my head kept spinning.

'Hey, Pascal,' I said, after a long time.

'Yeah?'

'Stop now. I feel great, but really, I don't need any more.'

His hands ceased moving and disappeared from my back. Left on its own, my skin began to tingle and I felt goosebumps rising up all over the place. Quickly, Pascal covered me with the doona, briefly resting a hand on my hair before I felt the bed shift as he stood up.

'You leaving?' I asked.

'I guess so.'

I felt him standing there, but neither of us said anything.

'You can sleep now, right?' he asked.

'Who knows.'

'So I'll leave you in peace?'

'You don't have to leave,' I said, impulsively. 'I don't want to talk or anything but you can stay for a while if you want to.'

Pascal sat back down beside me. Neither of us spoke. I kept my head buried deep in the pillow where it had lain since the massage began, too tired and loosened up to worry too much about anything. After another five minutes or so, Pascal lay down beside me.

'Is it all right?' he asked, quietly.

'Fine.'

I rolled over onto my back and looked up at the darkened ceiling. I probably should have been leaping out of my skin lying on the bed beside Pascal but we'd gone through too much that day for ordinary feelings to matter much.

Some time later — it could have been minutes, it could have been longer — I rolled onto my side and put an arm across his chest. It just seemed a natural thing to do. When he felt my touch he eased his arm under my head and there we lay until we both woke in the early hours of the morning, when Pascal climbed off my bed and hurried back to his room.

Chapter 6

There's no time to think about the meaning of romance when you've got an extremely meaningful appointment in the middle of a city you're totally unfamiliar with, at a quarter past nine in the morning. I woke up with a start, grabbed my watch and literally flew out of bed. It must have taken me fifteen minutes at the most to dress, put on some make-up, eat and run. Pascal wasn't with me. If there's one thing I can't stand, it's having someone hanging around watching me work — especially when I'm scared out of my tiny, wee brain.

I got to the back of the theatre at nine o'clock exactly and knocked on the large wooden stage door. It was opened by a woman about my age, who smiled at me and then had to stifle a wide yawn, exposing the soft pink of her mouth.

'Pretty early in the morning, eh?' Her nose wrinkled up in distaste.

I nodded.

'Come in.' She stepped aside and let me pass. 'The panel aren't here yet — neither are all of the actors but Sharon and I are. And, more to the point, we've got some hot coffee ready if you're interested. By the way, I'm Sophie. You must be Annie, right?'

'Right.'

I followed Sophie into a cavernous hall, with an old-fashioned stage and polished board floor. The air had the bite of autumn in it, but it would warm up in another hour or so. Sophie introduced me to Sharon and by the time we'd poured the coffee, a woman called Ilona and the two guys from the previous day's interview had arrived. By the time I sat down and pulled my script from my bag, the woman with the coloured hair had walked in, followed by two young guys she introduced as the other actors I'd be working with that morning. The woman in green wasn't coming — her son had broken his arm. I should have been sorry — both that her son had broken his arm and that she wouldn't see my work — but I hadn't liked her much, so the news brought a small smile to my nervous heart.

We drank coffee and talked until nine-thirty. More precisely, they talked and I drank coffee. No, I gulped coffee and my stomach fluttered and churned so loudly I was scared someone would hear me. I found myself wishing they'd call the whole thing off. I wondered how often there were bomb scares in the area, wished I was in Northern Ireland and then wondered whether there might be some chance of a fire drill intruding on the fast approaching session. I was saved in the end by the necessity of beginning. The old guy stood up, cleared his throat and introduced everyone. He told us all this stuff about how he knew how hard it was being put on the spot and how difficult it could be to have to work in front of a critical audience, and then he dragged his other two companions off into the shadows at the back of the hall to watch and wait.

The piece I had to direct was about a rodeo. They must have picked it as a test. And a test it was certainly going to be, to try to convince the three panel members that they were in the midst of a hot and dusty rodeo, up the top of Australia, when all I had to work with were the actors, five vinyl desk chairs, one table, a broom and a box full of old head scarves. I wondered whether the props had been selected for maximum difficulty or whether they were a random example of what you could expect to find back stage of any old theatre. I decided the panel wasn't that devious and that I was lucky to have any props at all.

The scene we had to produce involved five characters. Three white women — farmers — working the local hospital cake stall, a black cowboy, and a white guy about the same age as the cowboy. When Pascal and I had gone over the script the night before I'd had visions of directing it on a wide modern stage, with ochre scenery behind and sounds of the rodeo in the background. Of course I knew I wouldn't have those decorative touches to fill out the performance, but somehow I wasn't prepared for the emptiness of the hall, the cold air, and the five restless actors all staring at me, expectantly.

'Let's warm up,' I said, desperately.

I searched my mind for the exercises we used to do before we started work in Spain. I'd hated them at the time but I was beginning to see that a director has to be a bit like a school teacher with her actors. We had no music to dance to so I started clapping my hands as I called out to the actors instructions about what I wanted them to do. There was a clock above one of the hall doors and I kept them at it for a full five minutes before telling them to stop and take a few deep breaths. Before any of us had a chance to wonder whether I had any idea about where I was headed I got them playing a game we used to play as kids — British Bulldog. At least it warmed them up and got them laughing. After a noisy ten minutes I called them back.

'I don't like the feel of the stage.' I looked around me at the small area we had to work in. 'I'm going to move us down into the hall where there's a better feeling of space. We can push the chairs back to make enough room. David,' I looked at the guy who seemed to have the most energy to spare, 'I want you to play the cowboy.'

'Sure.' He smiled and began to walk off stage.

'No.' I held up a hand. 'I don't want you down in the hall. I'll call you when we're ready for you to work. You stay up there and wait.' I smiled at the others and waved for them to follow me.

I figured you had to do that sort of thing when you directed. You had to act a part yourself. I wanted David to be the black cowboy. In the story he was excluded and unwanted by the other characters so I'd decided to make it as easy as I could for him to play the part — and that meant leaving him out of what we were doing as a group. I glanced out of the corner of my eye and saw David sit himself down, cross-legged on the stage. I could tell he was watching us to see whether I was capable of carrying it off. I had to remember that he'd had some acting experience and I'd have to niggle seriously if I wanted to get under his skin. Just to make the feeling even stronger I gave the other four actors a whispering exercise to do — only this time I joined in too. After about ten minutes I stopped what we were doing and announced a quick read through the script. David went to climb down from the stage.

'You stay there,' I said, rudely. 'We don't want you yet. You don't have to read until about halfway through and you'll only get in the way.'

He sat back down and I couldn't help noticing his chest rise and fall with a sigh. I had to be careful that he didn't just get bored. I wanted him to be upset and on the edge of being angry. I decided I'd better bring him back into the group pretty soon and rely on being unkind to him to bring out the natural resentment I'd noticed.

'Okay.' I cleared my mind and smiled at the others. 'Take a seat everyone.'

We pulled the chairs into a circle.

'Sharon, you can be woman number one. Sophie, you can be the second woman. Ilona, I want you to be Daisy. And while you're reading,' I instructed her, 'I want you to feel David sitting up on the stage behind you, looking at you and listening to you, but remember you're very anxious not to let the other women know you're even aware of the cowboy's existence.'

'Tense, right?' She looked at me.

'Don't worry about looking tense, just feel it,' I said.

They got down to business and about halfway through their reading I called David into the circle, giving him my chair so he could become part of the group. I stood well back and let the actors get on with it without making any comments. They weren't as good as I'd hoped for but they were better than my worst fears had imagined. I wished I had somone I could trust to talk things through with though. Josh would have been best because he had a feel for working cooperatively with me, but right at that moment I would have settled for a helping hand from Pascal. I glanced up at the clock and noticed we'd only been at it for three quarters of an hour. I needed to fill up the time I'd been allotted without boring everyone senseless. I wondered if I should give the actors a break for coffee. I decided against it. I'd managed to forget the panel for a bit, but as the actors stopped reading, I could feel their judging eyes boring into my back.

'Okay,' I almost shouted, to break the sudden silence. 'I want to know what you thought about the way that sounded.'

We went through their opinions and thankfully, they had plenty of them, criticising each other and discussing the way the various parts could best be played. It was tempting to sit back and let it all happen but I made myself stay in the thick of things, having the last word on which approach the actors should take.

We broke for coffee after the first hour and a half and then worked on, steadily until I felt they were ready for the props to be introduced for our final performance. It was funny thinking we were about to make our 'opening night' performance in the empty hall, but that's what we had to do. I had to have the actors wanting to do their best for me. They needed to know I had confidence in them, but at the same time I couldn't afford to lose all the tension and emotion I'd worked so hard to develop. I began the build-up by working with them to set out the props. We used the broom as the rodeo barrier. Two vinyl chairs became horses in the arena. The women tied on head scarves to be hats against the blistering sun. The guys wore them around their necks like Western neckties. The scarf box became the cake stall and the other chairs we piled together to form a parked car for the white man to lounge against. In spite of the difficulties, there was an opening night excitement in the air and I think we all came close to forgetting it was around lunch time on an ordinary, everyday Wednesday afternoon. Finally, I called the actors to me and gave them a pep talk. I asked the panel members to come forward and make up the audience. Then, when they were all seated and the actors were waiting silently in their places, I stepped forward, introduced the play and described the scene.

I took my place to one side of the panel and did my best to watch the actors go through their paces. As far as I could tell they gave me their very best, but all of my sickening nervousness had returned about ten times over, and I couldn't really hear anything or see anything. My stomach groaned and churned. My head ached. My palms were cold and wet and my tongue felt dry and rough against my teeth. The play took a full ten minutes if not longer, but it felt to me as though I'd only just sat down and stopped fidgeting when the members of the panel began clapping. The next thing I knew, people were coming over, thanking me for the morning's work and disappearing out the door. I hobbled out after Sharon and vaguely computed the fact that the woman with the hair had just told me she'd found it all very interesting — whatever that was supposed to mean.

The plan had been for me to catch the tram back to Dad's friend's house, but Sharon took one look at me and insisted that she only lived around the corner from where I was headed and had nothing better to do than drive me home. I should have asked her what she thought my chances were, but it was all I could do to roll out of her car, wave goodbye and stumble in the front door of the house.

I slept for two hours and woke up to the sound of some soft and peaceful music. I thought it was Pascal being his thoughtful self again and hurried downstairs to tell him all about my morning's achievements. Instead, I found Dad's friend, reading on the couch.

'Oh,' I looked around for Pascal, but couldn't spot him. 'Hi. How are you?'

'Fine, Annie. How did it go?'

'All right I think.' I explained about vaguing out for the last part and then popped the question. 'Where's Pascal?'

'He's gone to visit the National Gallery and then I think he said something about shopping for presents for his family. He's a nice boy.'

'He is, isn't he?' I agreed.

'Do your parents know you're sleeping together?'

My mouth dropped open and I stared at her like a dying fish on the fishmonger's bench. 'Sleeping together?' The heat swept up my neck.

'Listen,' she shrugged. 'I've got no ambition to stick my nose into your affairs but I was asked to look after you both while you were in town and I'd be letting Ed and Jane down if I ignored what happened last night.'

'What are you talking about?' I forced the words out.

'I happened to get up in the night for a drink and the door to Pascal's room was open. Suffice it to say the bed was unslept in.'

Before I could say anything, she swept on with a carefully prepared speech.

'It's not that I'm bothered by the fact that you and your boyfriend are sleeping together. Hey, it's none of my business,' she spread her hands, 'I don't even know either of you. Still, it wouldn't be right to ignore the implications. I mean, are you using condoms? Have you thought your decision through properly? And I will add,' she fixed her eyes on me, 'that it's bad manners. I think you could have waited until you got home or alternatively, I should have been informed about the basis you two were visiting on. I understood you were friends and that was that.'

'You don't understand — '

'Oh yes I do,' she cut in. 'Sometimes, you young people think you're the only ones who've ever lived. I'm only forty years old. I know as well as you do about falling for guys and doing the business.'

'No, no,' I tried again, 'you don't know what

I'm saying. We didn't sleep together. I mean, we're not even going out. He just fell asleep in my room.'

'Oh yeah? And what was he doing in your room in the first place? I wasn't born yesterday, you know.'

'Nothing. I mean, he was giving me a massage.' I groaned and ran my fingers through my hair. 'It sounds pathetic, but it's true.'

'A massage?' she began to laugh. 'Oh, come on.'

'Did I choose a bad moment to walk in?' Pascal's voice sounded behind me.

I opened my mouth to explain and no words came out. Our host didn't help, she just shrugged her shoulders and looked over at me, expectantly. Pascal put his bags full of shopping down on the coffee table, and sat on the other end of the couch, waiting for me to say something.

'She thinks...' I coughed. 'She thinks we're sleeping together. I've tried to explain, but it sounds so... Well, you know.' I held open my hands.

Pascal coloured up so we made a matched pair

contrasting against the yellow couch.

'It wasn't like that.' Pascal looked down at his hands. 'Really it wasn't.'

She looked at him, carefully.

'Even if we wanted to, we couldn't,' he burst out. 'We're not both free — if you know what I mean. Annie and I are just very old friends. She had a really big day ahead of her and I wanted to help her sleep. It was nothing.'

'All right,' she sighed. 'I'll take your word for it. Many wouldn't, but I will. Just don't let it happen again, okay?'

We both shook our heads.

'No way,' I promised, my heart sinking a little. 'It'll never happen again.'

Chapter 7

Being back at home wasn't exactly comfortable. Pascal and I weren't saying much to each other — how could we? I was pretty devastated about what he'd said about not being free. I guess I should have known he'd have a girlfriend back in Spain but because he hadn't mentioned anyone in particular I'd just assumed he was on his own. I felt winded, like someone had knocked all the air out of me. All the way home on the plane I kept re-living that awful conversation, hearing Pascal explain why it wasn't possible for us to have been sleeping together. Weird that it took that to make me own up to the fact that I really did want to get back together with Pascal, even if it was only for a few lovely weeks. But now? Now all the moves I'd interpreted as being focused on me, turned out to be shyness. Maybe even nervousness around me in case I got the wrong idea.

I thought about that time we'd been on the couch together, the time he'd rubbed my feet between his hands — he was just being nice and I'd read everything into it. I shook my head and then hid my face in my pillow for a while. The good thing about being in your own room is that you can fall apart for a couple of minutes and you don't have to worry about anyone butting in and spoiling your self-pity. I thought about creeping out into the kitchen and calling up Leela. She'd be full of sympathy. She'd be able to offer me advice too, like whether I should ignore the fact that Pascal had a girlfriend or not.

Trouble was, Leela didn't even know I'd been chasing around after Pascal in my mind ever since I'd found him on my doorstep. I'd told her there was absolutely nothing doing. I'd told her the feeling wasn't there like it used to be when we were in Spain. I'd told her I wasn't interested in guys, that all I cared about was my film. I'd told her I was as excited about Pascal as I was about joining the girl guides. She'd fallen for it, hook, line and sinker. And now I was supposed to go back and admit I'd been keeping everything to myself? She'd think I wasn't much of a friend. I could understand it, but I didn't think she'd be too pleased. Besides, I wasn't in the mood for talking. I was in the mood for hanging around the house and sulking.

I sat up and swung my legs around so I was sitting up on my bed. My room was dark and poky and the posters I'd pinned up last year looked boring and daggy. I climbed onto my rickety desk chair and started ripping them down, crumpling them into balls of waste paper, picking at the bluetack left behind. What I needed was a white room. Clean, simple without any of this rubbish all over it. I stared at the stickers I'd stuck on the head of my bed about four years before. What was I doing living in a kid's bedroom? Well, things would be different now. I'd paint it all over. White walls, white curtains — I'd even paint the bed white. Turn it into the sort of room you could be in without thinking about guys. The sort of room someone who was too busy to waste time on men, would live in. Someone like me. A director's room. What did I need with a boyfriend, anyway? What good had they ever done anyone? I picked at the stickers, trying to tear away all the evidence of the past eighteen years and then I had a stunningly brilliant idea.

I headed out the back door and made a beeline for the garden shed. Along with about a kilo of spider webs and a mountain of oily dust, I turned up six sheets of sandpaper, a ladder, a paint scraper, a stiff old brush, a tin of undercoat and a plastic bucket. In the linen cupboard I scored two ripped sheets, a cloth beach hat, and some rags. I carried the lot into my room, put on an old pair of overalls, made a dash to the stereo to pump up the volume, and then got down to business. I pulled my bed into the hallway and spread out the sheets. The job didn't need to be perfect, so I sanded the walls pretty roughly and then opened up the nearly full can and started painting. I began near the window and managed to drip paint all over the alphabet curtains Mum and Dad put up when I was a kid — well, that sorted them out. The first wall didn't take too long. I didn't have to do the window frame because it was already white and only needed a wash, so I painted around it, trying to force myself to be sensible and not spill more paint than was strictly necessary. The curtains didn't matter, of course, but I didn't want to have to clean up all afternoon. I hummed to the music while I worked and didn't even mind the strain on my arms as I stretched to reach into the corners.

Next I tackled the roof, getting a fine spray of paint all over my face and hair. The first half of the roof was easy — awkward but easy. The second half was awful. I wasn't sure when it turned from fun into pain, but my neck began to hurt from looking up at the ceiling, the dull ache in my arms went white hot, and my back pleaded with me to stop. I made myself go on. By the time I got to the other three walls I'd slowed right down. Josh walked in as I stood facing the very last of them. At least with him there I felt I had to finish off the job — even if it was only to save my pride.

'You open for visitors?' He smiled at me, tentatively.

'Yes, so long as you're not here as a guy. I hate guys. They hang around messing everything up and ruining everyone's lives. I don't know where you think you're going to sit,' I glared at him, 'everything's covered.'

'I don't have to sit. I can stand.'

'Don't get in my way.'

'I wouldn't dream of it,' he said, moving into the far corner. 'What's the story with this "no guys allowed" business?'

'You heard. Only friends are welcome in my room.'

He stayed still in the corner for a couple of long minutes, stiff as a board, careful not to touch the walls behind him. Spots of wet paint circled where he stood on the drop sheets, and he eyed the area, uneasily. 'Maybe you'd like to step out for a while?' he suggested. 'I could make you coffee?'

'No,' I snapped.

'Okay, okay,' he nodded, standing up straighter than ever. 'I can deal with that. Can I at least bring in a chair to sit down?'

'You'd be more use if you helped,' I pointed out.

'My sweetest Annie,' he sighed. 'You know I'm not built for this sort of thing. Besides, it looks as though this is doing you the world of good. Nothing like hard work...' He grinned, wolfishly.

'What do you mean?' I glared at him.

'Just that this looks like some sort of out-pouring.' He waved his hands around the room. 'Anger, perhaps? Sorrow? Disappointment? What's it all about, or don't you want to tell dearest Josh?'

'There's nothing to tell.' I slapped my brush against the wall and a dollop of paint hit the floor, splattering my boot.

'Can I get you a rag?'

'If you want to stay, stay still. Don't talk to me or you risk being coated.'

He whistled through his teeth.

'Shut up, Josh.' I flicked the brush at him and

got him across the nose.

He jumped back and one of this elbows connected with the wet wall behind 'Annie!' he squealed. 'These are my good clothes. Now look what you've done.' He looked over his shoulder to assess the damage. 'Have I got paint on my jacket?'

'A bit.' I continued to paint.

'Will it come off?' he almost wept.

'Don't ask me. I wouldn't know.'

'Well, is it water paint?'

'I don't know.'

'You don't even know whether it's water paint?' He looked at me, scornfully.

'And you do, I suppose? I warn you, Josh,' I waved my brush at him, 'you're risking another flick, and I'll aim for your new pants this time.'

'No, no!' He held up his hands for mercy. 'Don't. I won't say another word.'

I turned back to my painting while Josh stood, silently watching me. It wasn't that bad having him there for company once he stopped teasing. I'd forgotten how soothing he could be when he wasn't competing with me for the limelight.

'Hey, Josh,' I called.

'What?' he replied, cautiously.

'What have you been doing with yourself, lately?'

'Nothing you don't know about.' He shrugged. 'I hung out with Izi when you were away in Melbourne, but I always hang out with Izi.' He paused. 'Oh, and we went to the movies with Leela and Sarah.'

'Sarah?' The name was unfamiliar.

'You don't know her,' he explained.

'I'm aware of that.'

'I only pointed it out because sometimes you forget you don't know everything.'

'Thanks for your kind words, Josh.'

'You don't have to be kind to your friends, only to strangers.' He smiled at me.

'You're rotten.'

'You see what I mean?' He grinned.

'So, what else?'

'Have I been doing, you mean?' he asked.

'Yeah.'

'Oh nothing much. Sarah and I went shopping this morning for a book she needed for her art history class.'

I felt the back of my neck tighten alarmingly. 'Are you trying to drop some heavy-handed hints in my direction, Josh? Because if you are, just get on with it and say whatever you have to say.'

'Such as?'

'Cut it out and tell me what's going on. Are you and this Sarah going out?'

'Got you!' he laughed. 'Jealous, eh? Feels awful, eh? Nasty thoughts, nasty sensations, eh?'

'I'm not jealous,' I protested.

'You are too. I saw the way the hair stood up on the back of your neck at the mention of her name.'

'Well, maybe I was a bit jealous,' I admitted.

'Right. Now you tell me,' he said, triumphantly, 'what's going on between you and Pascal?'

'*Nothing!*'

He whistled through his teeth for the second time. 'That sounds pretty powerful. What happened?'

'Nothing. I mean it. Nothing at all is going on, or has gone on between me and Pascal. Or will go on — if it comes down to it.'

'Pull the other one,' he sniffed.

'Okay, I admit it. I thought something was going on and maybe I was interested — '

'I knew it!'

'But he's not — interested, that is. He's got someone else, which is probably a good thing.'

'For me, it is,' Josh agreed.

'So you're still passionately, hopelessly infatuated with me?' I teased, not wanting things to get too heavy.

'Cross my heart.' He made the motions.

'Then you'll have to help me clean up.'

'I'm allergic to paint,' he moaned.

'And this from a guy who says he's in love. Who are you trying to kid?'

'It'll get on my clothes.'

'It's already on your clothes.'

'Only on the sleeve of my jacket, and that's bad enough.'

'So you'll have to be careful,' I said, stubbornly.

I surveyed my handiwork and then dropped the brush down into the empty paint tin. I moved the ladder over to the window, took down the curtains and threw them onto the wet floor. Josh stayed where he was, eyeing me, fearfully.

'Well?' I waited.

'Well, what?'

'Get moving and we'll chuck this lot out. Then you can help me get my bed back into the room.'

'Not fair,' he sighed.

'Just pull up your sleeves,' I instructed.

We rolled everything up into the ground sheets and took it all out to the bin. Josh dragged the bed back in and went off to make tea while I headed into the bathroom to wash up. Josh and I were easy together in a way I'd never been with Pascal. I could boss Josh around and he could do the same to me, and we both put up with it because we loved each other. I scrubbed at my hands, scratching at the paint, lifting the tiny spots with my fingernails. The only pity was, Josh didn't feel right as a boyfriend any more — and there was nothing I could do to change that. I picked up a face washer and cleaned off my face. The paint came off my skin all right, but I had it all through my eyebrows and my fringe looked as though it was made out of thick white twigs.

'Tea's ready,' Josh called, through the bathroom door.

'I'll be out in a minute. I can't seem to get this stuff out of my hair,' I grunted, trying desperately to dip my forehead into the tiny basin and loosen the paint's grip.

'Have a shower,' he suggested.

'Pass me a towel from the hall cupboard, will you?'

Josh slipped the towel through the door and I stepped under the water. The heat soothed my back and arms, and eased the white out of my eyebrows, but nothing seemed to work on my fringe. I washed it with soap, but that only made the white gleam whiter. I gave up eventually and went out to have my tea with Josh.

He was resting on my bed. He'd got it back into my room and had changed the sheets for me. Josh can't stand dirt, and he claimed I'd left footprints all over the sheets from when I'd moved the bed into the hall. I made him face the wall while I dressed — which felt pretty strange. There was a time, not so long ago when I wouldn't have worried. I would've felt comfortable getting dressed in front of Josh. The memory jumped through me and I hurried into my clothes, trying to chase it away. The last thing I wanted was to confuse the way I felt about Josh. We were friends and that was one of the good things in my life. No boyfriends, I reminded myself. I'm happy the way I am.

'What are you muttering about?' Josh turned around.

'Don't look!' I spun about and faced the wall. 'I'm not ready.'

'Hurry up then. Your tea's getting cold.' I heard him pat the spot beside him.

I finished buttoning my shirt and turned around to face him. His hair fell over his forehead and his cheeks looked soft and full. I remembered kissing those cheeks. I love Josh's face. It's the sort of face you can spend hours dreaming about... I sighed out loud and realised I'd been mooning over Josh! At least he hadn't seen and couldn't read my mind. It was probably just this business with Pascal that had set me dreaming. Feeling sorry for yourself could be dangerous when it got out of hand. I went over and sat down on the bed. Josh smiled and reached past me to hand me my cup. Our legs touched and to my horror I felt a shock go through me. Josh flicked a smile in my direction and that too hit home. I moved up the other end of the bed and took a good, big sip of hot tea.

'Come on, Annie,' he said. 'You don't have to keep your distance. Who cares about whether we should or shouldn't go out together, and whether you want Pasacal or you don't? I'm here. I'm your friend. We can enjoy each other's company without it meaning anything major.'

I slid back down to Josh's spot on the bed and he put one of his big arms around me. I knew it was crazy but I leant forward and kissed him, softly. The edge of his smiled curled up, making his cheeks as round as apples and he whispered his lips against my skin. It felt wonderful. But I didn't want to go out with Josh again. No way. That was finished. It was all over between us. I pulled back and picked up my tea, trying to act like nothing had happened.

'What's the matter?' he asked.

'Nothing. Forget it.'

'Come on, Annie, relax. It's okay to care about

me still.'

'Yes, but...' I groaned.

'But nothing. Why don't we give it another try? What's so bad about us being together? I know you like me. Why won't you give me a chance?'

'Don't, Josh,' I pleaded. 'Don't talk like that. We're friends and you'll wreck everything if you keep carrying on with all that stuff.'

'So there's no way?' He looked at me, carefully.

I shook my head.

'Then at least come back over here and give me a farewell hug.'

I moved closer again and we put our arms around each other. He felt warm and comfortable against me, even if the occasion was a bit sad.

'Annie?' He cleared his throat.

'Yeah?'

'If it was just today? If we were just together, here in your room for the afternoon, and you didn't have to worry even for a moment about me thinking it meant anything more, would you want to be with me?'

'Don't, Josh! You're making me feel awful.'

'I'm serious.'

'How can you be serious about such an idiotic idea? It's stupid. It's not going to happen, so what's the point in even talking about it?'

'Why not? We're both lonely. We both love each other. Why shouldn't we be together if we agree it's no big deal?'

'You're not talking about actually doing it, are you?'

'Not specifically. Why, do you want to or something?'

'God no.'

'Well you don't have to make it sound like it's such a revolting idea.'

'I never said that,' I snapped.

'Good,' he sulked.

'But I don't want to have sex with you.'

'And I don't want to have sex with you either,' he insisted.

'Bull!'

'What do you mean, bull?' He moved away from me.

'Just that I bet you do.'

'Do what?' He raised an eyebrow.

'Want to have sex with me,' I said, feeling a

blush sweep over my face.

'Why? Because you're so gorgeous?'

'No,' I bit my lip and wished I'd never opened my big mouth. 'Come on, Josh. Don't give me a hard time.'

'You think just because I'm a guy I automatically want to have sex the whole time.'

'No...' I tailed off.

'Well you're wrong anyway. I wouldn't want to even if you did. Not unless you wanted to go out with me again.'

'But I don't.'

'Right,' he nodded. 'So let's just forget that, and get back to where we were before you so rudely brought all this up.'

'It wasn't rude,' I complained. 'I was being sensible.'

'Okay,' he shrugged, 'before you so sensibly brought the subject up.'

'And where were we, before that?' I relaxed.

'You were sitting right up close to me...'

I moved over beside him.

'And I suggested that we should pretend we're all alone in the world — that there's no tomorrow...'

'Josh,' I laughed, 'you're so corny.'

'But you adore me.' He grinned.

'I do,' I agreed. 'Mind you, it's a pretty dumb idea.' I warmed to the thought. 'I'll probably regret it later.'

'Maybe, but so what? It's not as if I'm some stranger and we'd end up thinking rotten things about each other. There's a chance I might regret it too but at least I'll know it was with you, and if we promise...'

'Yeah, but it feels silly now we've talked about it. I might laugh.'

'Doesn't matter.' He shook his head. 'You can laugh if you want, I won't care. Let's just have fun and cheer ourselves up a bit.'

'I feel embarrassed.'

'That's all right.' He beamed, happily. 'So do I.'

'Will you stop telling me everything's all right all the time?' I complained. 'It's annoying. It's one of the things about you that just drives me crazy.'

'Let's quit talking and get down to business,' he suggested.

'You're outrageous, Josh.'

'Well, if we don't, the day will be over before we've had a chance to do anything we'll regret later on — and it's always good to have something worth thinking about.'

'Okay,' I laughed and opened my arms, 'come over here.'

We lay down on my bed and carried on like a couple of complete kids. We'd kiss for a bit and get right into it, then one of us would think of something we just had to tell the other, and we'd rave away until one of us would complain about all the time we were wasting on talking. It went around and around in circles. I guess it was about when I was lying right on top of Josh, when he had his top off and I was seriously considering doing the same with mine, that Pascal decided to pay me a visit. He gave a tiny tap at the door, but didn't wait for my answer. I guess he wasn't expecting me to say I was busy. I remember hearing something and beginning to move off Josh so I could turn around and see what it was, and then the next thing I knew Pascal had walked right in. He stood in front of the door with the most awful look of embarrassment all over his face. Josh and I flew apart like opposite poles of a magnet, and I remember grabbing at my mug of cold tea like I'd been about to get on with drinking it only Josh had distracted me.

'Sorry,' Pascal stammered.

'No, no. It was nothing,' I insisted, bravely. 'We were just... We were just... Well, it wasn't really what you're thinking. Ummm. Josh, er... How can I put it?'

'We were discussing the meaning of the universe,' Josh piped up.

'Shut up, Josh!' I snapped.

'Please,' Pascal backed towards the door, 'it's none of my business. Don't apologise.'

'But...' I looked about me desperately for inspiration. 'I — We're old friends.'

'Yes,' Pascal looked at us both, 'I can see that.'

Chapter 8

I was going to run after him. I would've abandoned poor, old Josh and chased after Pascal if I could have thought of what to say, but I couldn't. I suppose someone else might've been able to explain that scene with Josh away, but even the thought of seeing Pascal again sent red waves flying across my cheeks and I hated to think what colour I'd turn if I actually had to speak to him. But I didn't have to — not that day anyway. I stayed in my room with Josh for a bit talking things over, and when I did come out, Pascal had left for the evening — which made me feel more desperate than ever.

I invented this speech I was going to make. I was going to tell him that although he probably wasn't interested, I needed to explain that Josh wasn't my boyfriend, that it was important to me that he knew Josh and I had completely finished with each other, that we were just saying goodbye, and I hoped he'd be able to believe me.

Trouble was, when I saw Pascal the next day, the words died on my lips. I mean, how do you set about telling someone the state of your lovelife when theoretically, it's none of their business? It would've been different if Pascal was interested in me and he'd let me know about it, then I'd have had some reason to bring the subject up, but as it was... No, there was nothing I could do. There was nothing I could say. To explain anything would be to make a total fool of myself — in front of the guy I was trying to convince how fabulous, cool and sophisticated I was!

And what about Josh? I wasn't too pleased with him. I wasn't feeling sorry for him, anyway. He was supposed to be my best friend in all the world and he'd messed up my whole life — probably ruined it forever. Probably, I'd never go out with anyone again. I couldn't imagine going out with anyone ever again, not now that I felt so sure Pascal was the one and only love of my life. I'd probably have to become a nun — maybe even devote my life to saving some almost extinct species of earwig that nobody cared about anyway. And my romantic future? I didn't want to even think about that.

All the same, I spent the next week having the most ridiculous fantasies about running off to Spain with Pascal. Sometimes he'd walk into my room with two tickets, throw them down on the bed, and demand I spend the rest of my life with him. Sometimes I'd storm into the spare room, tell him I loved him desperately, and together we'd head off for the travel agent's. My favourite was the one where he went back to Spain without me, I turned around and sold my film for a small fortune and then followed him over there to set up my own movie studio — which would become fantastically famous and successful. I'd arrive at the airport, catch a cab to the university, and walk right up to him as he strolled across the campus grounds. It always ended with us throwing our arms around each other. I tried working on the idea that he stayed in Australia after falling at my knees and confessing he couldn't live without me, but I found the idea of staying where I was pretty boring. Eventually, I settled on a version where we flew to Spain but had to wander the world to escape our irate parents. No need to dwell upon the fact that the more out of hand my imagination got, the more embarrassed I became in front of the guy himself. How are you supposed to act naturally in front of someone you've just imagined yourself running away with? You can't. The best you can do is try to act cool — which is what I did.

Thank God I had the film. The film gave me a reason to speak to Pascal without having to say anything about anything. The film gave me a chance to be around him without feeling stupid or going red all day long. And the film gave me and Josh something to do while we worked out how we were going to get along together after what had happened between us.

Most importantly of all, the film was my escape. That is, it was my escape until it got a life of its own and started to mean more to me than either Pascal or Josh rolled into one.

I threw myself into it. I got Josh writing. I got Izi sitting down, sorting out his equipment and reading up about the best way to work the lighting. And I got Pascal and my other actors rehearsing. Funny the way things seem to weave in together. I'd never intended to make them rehearse. I didn't think it was necessary. I'd thought I had all the time in the world to make the film. A messed-up scene had meant another shoot and who cared? But now I had to send something down to Melbourne for assessment, everything had to be spot-on the first time around. And the only way I could be sure that the actors knew what they were doing before we started the video rolling, was to make them rehearse each scene the way I'd made the actors rehearse for the performance I'd directed before the selection panel in Melbourne.

I began to see that it really did make sense to do a course. Anyone could make a film, but hardly anyone could make a good film. I wanted to make good films. No, that wasn't strictly true. I wanted to make excellent films — great films. The sort of films that blew people away. The sort of films that sent you racing off to Hollywood to make a million or two when you were still only nineteen. I'd be in *New Idea*, *TV Week*, *Who* — maybe even *Time* magazine. The future was limitless and my idea about becoming a nun faded deep into the background.

My family hated it. Mum and Dad had been so excited that I'd found something to do but they weren't prepared for how seriously I was taking things. I think Mum thought taking a week off work was going to be a bit of a holiday, but she was wrong. I made everyone involved get up at five o'clock each morning for a six o'clock start. I think I was as fanatical about the film as the characters were about their netball.

All the same, it wasn't all my fault that we had to have such early starts. A certain young writer had to accept some of the responsibility too. Josh had written six quick flashes of the netball family's morning workouts, and he wanted Izi and I to edit them into the main storyline. But the actors didn't take it out on Josh, did they? They took it out on me! We worked on those scenes four mornings in a row. Dad, alias Herman, ran around the court, a silver whistle about his neck shouting at Aileen and the girls as the ball shot from one set of cold, wet hands to another, rapid fire. It was meant to be early morning — before school, before breakfast even — and there had to be frost on their breaths and dew on the grass around the edge of the court. I wanted Aileen, Darleen, Rayleen, Doreen and Colleen to be steaming with exertion, their bare legs had to be red with effort while their upper arms fought the chill air with goose bumps two centimeters high. Dad complained about the conditions and he was one of the lucky ones, he got to wear a nylon tracksuit. Mum, Pascal and the others had to nip about the court in sports tunics, runners and ankle socks. By the third day they weren't speaking to me. They'd finish a scene and instead of hanging around and giving me advice like they used to when we first started, they'd disappear into Mum's car, roll up the windows and glare at me through the mist on the windows. I wasn't popular — and that was putting it mildly. The only person who had anything nice to say to me was Pascal and I figured that was probably only because he didn't know me well enough to be awful to me. Like Josh said, you're rude to your friends and nice to strangers. What a world!

In my heart of hearts I wasn't exactly happy. Surprise, surprise, eh? But it wasn't just because everyone was annoyed with me about the film. I wouldn't have minded that. Well, I sort of wouldn't have minded it... If it were just the film, I would've told myself to put it down to professional experience and avoid working with family and friends in the future. So it wasn't being everyone's enemy that was eating me up. It was all that stuff that'd gone on with the guys in my life. I felt so guilty about having fooled around with Josh when I knew perfectly well it meant far more to him than it did to me — at least, that's what I thought sometimes. But just when I started feeling like that, another part of me would pipe up and start defending me, and

I'd be carrying on about how inconsiderate Josh had been and how he should have thought about my feelings and my life.

There was this regular war going on in my head — Josh shouldn't have fooled around with me versus I shouldn't have fooled around with Josh. And all this while I was trying to work — while I was trying to concentrate! Then there was Pascal to think about. Of course it was all over between us. Our romance didn't stand a chance. Not that anything had started, but now nothing ever would. Sometimes it seemed as though that was how it was supposed to be. But another part of me said I should push things along a little, go and make that speech after all — just to see what happened.

I wished I had someone to talk to. I'd gotten past just thinking about confiding in Leela. I'd actually fronted up and told her about everything but it hadn't helped. It'd only made me even more miserable. I talked to Leela before I realised how annoyed everyone was with me about the film. Not that she said anything. She was nice enough. She said all the things a friend should say. She told me I was right, that I was the best, that the guys didn't know how lucky they were, and that Pascal was showing every sign of being in love with me, but it didn't ring true. She wasn't being herself. She kept giving me these sideways looks and slipping in comments about trying not to come on too strong with people, about how 'people' could get put off by my manner if they didn't know me like she knew me. When you start hearing stuff like that it makes you think twice about coming back for more.

But finally, a week after my trip to Melbourne, something went right for once in my life. I got to slip the videotape of the film into an express bag and post it down to the selection panel. I felt like I should've put a spell on the thing to give me luck, but I didn't know any spells and besides, I don't believe in that sort of stuff. In the end I just sighed and sealed it up. I told myself you couldn't do much except try your best, the rest was all luck and talent. And I *had* tried my best. That video contained so much work. Izi and I had slaved over the final edit until four in the morning. Each night of that week I'd fallen into bed totally exhausted. My family weren't talking to me. Josh had run off with Sarah. Leela wasn't returning my calls. And all I had was this piece of black plastic sealed in a yellow express bag. God, I hoped it was worth it. I handed it over the counter and watched the clerk slip it into a calico sack.

The next three days were like the days I'd spent waiting to hear about course offers. I had nothing to do because the film was finished. I didn't really want to do anything because I was too busy waiting. And time seemed to stretch out forever. Mum and Dad went back to work, and apart from Pascal I could have been alone on the planet. When the phone actually rang and I heard the STD pips, I think I went into shock. It was as though I'd been waiting all that time to hear nothing, to get some old letter telling me thanks, but no thanks — only that didn't happen. They called me. They weren't calling to offer me a place exactly, but to ask me to come back down for a second interview.

There I was holding the phone against my

ear, listening to the old guy say all this stuff about how impressive my film was, about how they hadn't seen anyone of my age with my confidence around actors I'd never met before, about how they normally preferred older students and about how they wanted me to come down and meet some big wig who could authorise a special additional place in their course. They weren't offering me anything definite because they'd already ruled me out of the limited places they had available, but when they'd received my film they'd decided to make an exception. I just held on to the phone and mumbled some stuff about how grateful I was. I don't know what I actually said, but I did agree to fly down the next day.

Pascal found me sitting in my favourite spot on the couch, just staring into space. It took about five minutes before he managed to get the full story out of me and it took about another ten minutes before he convinced me I hadn't imagined the whole thing, that he'd definitely heard the phone ring, and that he'd noticed I'd spent a long time talking to someone who'd had a lot to say.

'But how am I going to get there?'

He laughed. 'You just told me you're flying down tomorrow.'

'Yeah, but with what money? How? I haven't even got a seat on the plane. What if they're booked out? I bet they're booked out. Oh God,' I groaned. 'They're booked out.'

'Everything will be fine. Ed and Jane will give you the money. Your parents haven't been running around that netball court for fun, you know. They want this for you.'

'But what if there aren't any seats?'

'There will be.' He nodded, confidently.

'But how do you know? There mightn't be.'

'Then you can take the train. But there will be,' he added.

'How long does the train take? I might miss the interview. Did I say what time it was? Oh no, I've forgotten.' I looked about me, desperately. 'What am I going to do? I'll have to ring them back and they'll think I'm hopeless. They won't want someone in their course who can't remember what time to turn up for an interview.'

'Take it easy. Think it over. What did they say?'

I thought it through and then realised I'd written everything down on the pad near the phone. I started up from the couch and dashed into the kitchen.

'Here it is,' I called. 'Two in the afternoon. At the college. First floor. I go to the reception desk and ask for the dean's office. The dean?' I pulled up sharply. 'That's pretty heavy, isn't it? Boy, I don't know if I can handle this.' I carried the notepad back into the sitting-room. 'Do you think I can handle it?'

'Of course. Don't be silly.'

'What time will the plane get in?'

'You're asking me?' He made a face. 'I'm the tourist, remember?'

'I should ring, I guess?'

'Yeah,' he smiled, 'and then call your parents. Maybe your dad can organise us some accommodation.'

'Us? Are you coming? What for? I won't be doing anything exciting. I'm just going there for the interview.'

'You need someone to take care of you.'

'No I don't.' I shook my head.

'Yes you do,' he enthused. 'You've been working so hard. And after what happened with Josh and Sarah, well...' He stopped and looked embarrassed.

'What do I care about Josh and Sarah?'

'Sorry, I shouldn't have mentioned it.' Pascal went a bit red. 'I didn't mean to bring that up. I know it's private. It's none of my business really, but I thought it was really rotten of him to do it to you — especially in the middle of filming.'

My jaw dropped. 'Pardon?'

'He could have waited.' Pascal shrugged and looked embarrassed.

'But it's great. Josh needs someone to love him — and she adores him.'

He eyed me, strangely. 'That's very generous of you. Maybe I just don't understand what's going on. You see, I thought... I, ah...' He blushed. 'The other day when I, ah, came into your room... I guess I just jumped to conclusions.'

Now I started blushing. 'Oh, of course! I was going to explain — '

'Explain, you don't have to explain,' he burst out. 'It's none of my business.'

'I know but I wanted to tell you about Josh, only I didn't know what to say.'

'You don't have to tell me anything.' He backed away.

'Pascal, please. Sit down. Maybe I'll regret this later but we've got some talking to do so just stop all this stuff about whether it's anyone's business or not. There's just one thing though,' I held up my hand as Pascal began to lower himself into his seat, 'you'd better drop this stuff about coming to Melbourne to look after me. I don't need that sort of help from you. Maybe I do want something, but it's not being looked after.'

'What is it then?'

'Just hang on a minute.' I plonked myself down beside him. 'I'm not up to that part yet.'

My prepared speech rolled off my lips and into the air between us in a matter of seconds. Pascal bit the corner of his lip and looked down at the couch, just taking it all in. At first I thought I was doing the wrong thing in telling the whole story of me and Josh, and the heat began to creep up my face, but then I saw a smile on his face and he lifted his eyes and looked into mine.

'I don't know what you're so happy about,' I complained. 'It was awful. It was the worst moment of my life.'

'Why?'

'Why?' I squealed. 'How can you ask why? How would you like being walked in on by someone who didn't know what was really going on?'

'I would have been embarrassed,' he shrugged, 'but it wouldn't have been the worst moment in my life. No way! Maybe I wouldn't even have cared about what the person who walked in thought.'

'I did.'

'Why?' he asked again.

'I don't know.' I looked into his eyes and then glanced away.

'Please tell me why.'

I stood up. 'How about a celebratory drink? Let's go down to the pub and buy some cider. No, maybe champagne would be best — only I don't really like it all that much. Have you got any money? Because I'm dead broke.'

'I think so.' Pascal stood up and felt in his pocket. 'Ten dollars. I'll take you for a drink.'

'Great,' I led the way into the hall. 'I'll just call the airline. I'll book the flight and we can tell Mum and Dad about it later, when they get home.' I walked into the kitchen and dialled the number. 'Hey, you!' I called out into the hall.

'What?' Pascal answered.

'Are you serious about coming?'

'Book two seats. I won't get in your way. I promise.'

I don't drink much, I only have a glass now and again when I really feel like it. Not that I've had years of experience, I've only been old enough to go into bars for a little while and hanging out in pubs isn't really my scene. But our local has a really nice beer garden — Josh and I used to hang out there a bit.

Pascal and I walked down to the hotel and sat out in the garden. We bought two bags of chips and two glasses of beer. Our pub isn't trendy so they don't give you little plates of things to nibble with your drink. It's more a case of the barman throwing a packet of chips in your direction and getting back to the serious business of watching the races the minute your drink is poured. It didn't worry us though. We were the only people in the garden and we liked it that way. We got the best seat, under the warm autumn sun. I opened up my chips, had a sip of beer, and made myself comfortable.

I'd thought we'd talk about stuff. I'd thought we were getting pretty close to saying something about something, to telling each other we were interested and that kind of thing. Only now, we were there, sitting in the garden without any interruptions, we didn't say a word. We munched chips, we sipped beer, we sighed and stretched, Pascal took off his jumper and tied it around his waist, I looked up at the clouds, we both swatted at the European wasps hovering about our feast, but we didn't say anything.

I gave Pascal a quick glance and noticed how gorgeous he looked. Maybe I could talk about Spain? I thought about it but decided it was too far in the past. I thought about the film but it was too boring. I considered discussing our accommodation in Melbourne but that was too scary. There really wasn't anything I could say. I munched another chip, sipped my drink, and watched the way Pascal's arm muscles shifted when he lifted his drink. A blush crept up my face. I willed it to leave. I shifted in my seat and swivelled around a little. I hung my head and let my hair fall over my face.

'What's the matter?' he asked.

'This seat's so uncomfortable,' I lied. 'Let's go. Let's get out of here.'

He followed me out through the bar and on to the street. I was in the middle of one of the happiest days of my life and all I could do was waste my time mooning over a guy. Stupid, eh? I strode along the footpath, letting Pascal struggle to keep up with me.

'What's wrong?'

'Nothing.'

'You're upset,' he insisted.

I gritted my teeth. 'I'm not upset.'

'Annie, stop it.'

He put his hand on my arm, and pulled me back until I'd stopped walking. I didn't look up, just stared at the pavement and wondered what on earth I was going to do to get out of this one. Being with Pascal was even more difficult than being with Josh.

'Would you please tell me what's going on?' he pleaded.

'You really don't know?' I met his eyes.

'I'm not sure.'

'Well neither am I,' I agreed.

'But say it anyway.' He put a hand on my shoulder. 'Please.'

'I don't know how,' I groaned. 'What am I supposed to say? Why does it always have to be me who has to come out and say everything?'

'It wasn't you last time,' he frowned, 'it was me.'

'You?' I stared at him. 'You didn't say anything. Not that I remember. You just sat there on the couch and put your arm around me, then your sister walked in and I nearly jumped out of my skin.'

'Well if I didn't say anything, at least I started it. Now it's your turn. It's only fair.'

I smiled and felt my whole body relax. 'Okay,

I'll start it.' I leant over and touched his lips with mine. Just a soft touch but we both felt it in every little part of our bodies. 'Oh boy,' I groaned, 'this is so dumb. We've got the worst timing. You're going soon. I'm going soon. Why aren't you here for a year so we can have a decent time together? There,' I sighed, 'I've said it. Now can we go home?'

Pascal put his hands up to my face and moved my hair back from my cheeks. 'Can I come to Melbourne with you?'

'We already agreed on that.'

'Shall we sneak off on our own?'

'Not stay with Dad's friend?'

Pascal smiled.

'You're nothing but trouble,' I poked him in the ribs. 'Not this time. This trip is for work, not for fun or for getting into trouble with my parents. If you were staying around, maybe, but my life's complicated enough as it is.'

Mum and Dad didn't notice anything strange about us when they arrived home that evening. The phone call from Melbourne was enough to explain my sudden mood change, and they seemed to think it was natural that Pascal should want to fly down with me. So for the second time we found ourselves on the plane, and then catching a bus and a tram out to St Kilda. It was nine o'clock in the evening by the time we arrived though. Mum hadn't wanted me running short of time and had insisted we change our booking and fly down that night so I wouldn't be too stressed for the interview the next day.

Dad's friend was expecting us. She had our rooms made up and had made us some supper in case we were hungry. It wasn't an exciting evening really. I was too edgy thinking about the interview and Pascal and I were keeping about a kilometre apart, not wanting to arouse any suspicion about our relationship. All the same, it was lovely being there, watching Pascal and knowing we both felt the same way. There's something about that first moment when you start going out with someone — everything's sweet, everything's wonderful and everything's ahead of you.

Chapter 9

'**W**hat a pleasure it is to meet you.' The dean held out her hand. 'So you're the young woman everyone is so excited about.'

I blushed.

'Perhaps we could get down to business?' suggested the younger guy from the panel. 'Annie is flying home today so we've only got her for a little while. We wanted you to have a chance to speak to her yourself, Professor Mills. We think she'd be an asset to the college, despite her age.'

'I'm sorry we're harping on about your youth.'

The dean looked down at me from a great height. 'We're cautious about accepting anyone under twenty, you know. We've tried it in the past and it rarely works. It's not an easy course. We're maintaining extremely high standards and our students work on a professional level. This degree is the most sought after of its kind, so we have a reputation to uphold.'

'I'd like to be given a chance,' I said.

'I'm sure you would,' she smirked, 'but there is a great deal of work involved. The hours — '

'We've explained about the hours,' the guy cut in. 'We're convinced she could manage — '

'Well, I'd like to hear that from Annie herself,' the dean cut back, sharply.

I looked from one to the other. The dean sat down behind her desk. Her face was carefully made up. Her pink nails reflected the tiny brass paper weight, resting in front of her hands, and she pursed her lips with disdain. The guy from the panel sat beside me in a lounge-chair. He seemed to sink into the soft cushioning and looked uninspiringly small sitting in front of the dean's expansive desk. I didn't think we had much chance.

'Did you like my film?' I asked, suddenly.

'Roger?' The dean looked at the guy from the panel.

'A short film Annie sent in,' he explained.

'It's only ten minutes long,' I pulled a copy out of my bag. 'Why don't we look at it and then you can ask me whatever you like. The film might give you more of an idea about whether I'm the sort of student you're looking for.'

'Yes.' The dean smiled for the first time. 'Good suggestion. Can we organise a player?' She turned to Roger. 'I think you'll find one in the outer office.'

Roger skipped out of the room and left us on our own.

'I hope it's not one of those films without any story.' The dean looked worried. 'I like a strong narrative line. I like to understand what I'm watching.'

'It's got a story, but it is only a short film. I mean, you can't get too involved in something that only runs for ten minutes.'

'Well, we'll soon see.' The dean looked up as

Roger wheeled in the video player.

I handed over the cassette and watched as he slipped it into the slot, and pressed play. I crossed my fingers and wished Roger would turn out the lights so I wouldn't have to witness the dean's reaction. Just my luck to run across someone who liked conservative films when mine was about something as crazy as a netball family and a boy in drag, and had hardly any dialogue apart from stuff about on court strategy. I crossed my fingers, sat on my hands and forced myself to watch. For the first few minutes we sat in total silence. Then I heard a small sound beside me. I thought the dean might be getting restive — either too bored or too outraged to sit through the film quietly, but she moved again and I heard a giggle escape her. Soon there were outright laughs coming from both Roger and the dean. Not from me though. I was too nervous. I sat on my crossed fingers — figuring you couldn't be too careful. As the screen reverted to static, I turned around to face her and receive my sentence.

'I play a little netball.' She looked at me, enthusiastically. 'Well, I used to. I'm a bit too old now and I have some trouble with my knees, but my two daughters play. My oldest, Melissa is trying for the state team. She'd like this film. I'm always on to her about training, about playing intelligently. I should take this home and show her. She'd love it. Of course we're not netball fanatics,' she said, hurriedly. 'I don't mind whether the girls play or not, but I've made it clear to them right from an early age that it's in their own interests to play hard. Apart from anything else it's a great way to make friends. You play?'

'No.' I shook my head. 'I prefer tennis.'

'Tennis is all right,' the dean mused, 'but not like netball. There's something special about netball. We've been playing for four generations in my family.'

'Take it home.' I handed over my copy. 'I've got plenty more.'

'Really?' She looked delighted. 'That's very kind of you. I'll tell the girls I've just accepted the film's director into our course.'

'Accepted?' My mouth dropped open.

'Oh yes.' The dean's face became serious again.

'You're outstanding. By all means we'll make a place for you. Roger,' she turned to the panel member. 'I don't know why you were so hesitant. Honestly, you have to start making these decisions for yourself. I can't always be bothered sorting out your department's problems. But, enough of that! Annie doesn't want to listen to my administrative headaches. Roger, I want you to help Annie organise her enrolment before she goes home this evening. And can't we do something about her accommodation?' The dean spread her hands wide. 'If we're going to be taking someone of her age from interstate then she needs a bit of support to find housing.'

'I could take her down to student housing.'

'Yes, yes of course,' the dean snapped. 'But don't we have some flats for rural students?'

'I'm not sure.'

'Well, go and find out. Go on, go on.' She waved Roger out of his seat. 'We want Annie to be able to go home and give her parents some idea about what she's getting in to. Tell Shirley down in student admin that I want us to help all we can. She'll fix something up.' The dean stood up and held out her hand to me. 'It's been lovely meeting you. I hope you'll find time over the next three years to drop in and let me know how you're going.'

'Thank you,' I said. 'Thank you. You won't regret this.'

'I never regret anything,' she said.

Chapter 10

For the next two weeks Pascal and I stuck together like glue. I thought I was crazy about him when we went out together in Spain but this time I really was in love.

After we arrived home from Melbourne we sat down and made plans. Pascal hadn't done much sightseeing because he'd been too busy helping with the film and I hadn't had much fun since leaving school because I'd been too busy being depressed about the future and then too busy directing the film. Now seemed to be the right moment to make up for lost time — not to mention the fact that my parents were feeling particularly generous with me after my success.

We spent three days visiting anything worth seeing in a thirty kilometer radius around our town. Then we borrowed Dad's car and drove up to Queensland, camping along the way. It was a total surprise to me to be allowed that much freedom but my parents said that if I was going to live in Melbourne on my own then I was obviously able to handle a bit of touring with a guy they both really liked and knew quite well. And it was good. It was wonderful being out of home, on our own, doing what we felt like doing. I think that's when Pascal got his great idea — only he didn't say anything then. He didn't even hint that he'd concocted a plan. I had no idea about what was coming until the day before Dad and I were set to leave.

The dean managed to get me on some priority list as a country student and the college offered me a room in a house just across the park from the college itself. I wasn't wild about the idea of having to share with three other strangers but no matter where I went I was going to have to face up to meeting new people. It was strange to think I'd have to sleep in a new house, on a new bed, with bedroom furniture I'd never seen before when I'd spent my whole life in the same room, in the same house, with all the same stuff. It made me nervous. I was nervous about organising everything. I was nervous about how I'd go setting up house. And when Dad offered to drive down and spend the first week helping me settle in, it was as though someone had lifted a death sentence from me. That was, until Pascal piped up with his news.

'I'm going to come too.' He beamed at me.

'You're what?' I stopped packing my black jumper into my suitcase and stared at him.

'I'm coming. It's a surprise.'

'What are you talking about?'

'I knew you wouldn't want to do this on your own so I changed my ticket, and now I'm coming with you.'

He walked over and put his arms around me.

'Oh, Annie,' he sighed. 'I can't leave you. These two weeks have been like nothing else in my life. I know it sounds strange but I feel I'm alive when I'm with you. Now I can't imagine ever being away from you. Besides, what's Western Australia to me? Sure I wanted to go there before I went home but that was before I saw you and realised how much you meant to me.'

'But, Pascal, everything's arranged.'

'We'll just un-arrange it.'

'But I'm travelling with Dad.'

'I like your old man,' he laughed. 'We get on well.'

'But that's not the point,' I said.

'So?' he waited.

'Well, it's just… It's just I wasn't prepared for this. I had it sort of fixed in my mind that we were saying goodbye tomorrow…'

'I thought you'd be pleased.'

'Of course I am,' I snapped. 'Of course I want to spend some more time with you but I just hadn't planned on it.'

'But you want to?'

'Yeah,' I shrugged. 'I guess so.'

'You don't sound very enthusiastic.'

'I am. It's only…'

'What?' he asked.

'Oh, Pascal,' I sighed, 'why did you have to go and mess everything up? Everything was perfect and now you've ruined it.'

'I don't understand.' He sank down onto the edge of my bed.

'What's the point in you coming to Melbourne? Seriously, what's the point? I can see it's good for you. You get to be with me and you get to know the city a bit better, but apart from that it doesn't really change anything for you. You still go off home after another couple of weeks.'

'But I have to. I've got my course. I'm part-way through and I can't just dump it now.'

'I know that. And I'm not asking you to.'

'Then what's the problem?'

'The problem is, I've got *my* course to think about. I've got Dad with me for a week while I settle in but then that's it! Then I start studying and you're... what? You're going to walk me to class and back? And where are you going to stay? And how about me having to be with you when I'm in the middle of meeting the people I'm going to be living with. I don't want my attention divided.'

'I thought you loved me,' he said.

'Well, I *do*. But that's not the point.'

'Isn't that the most important thing, that we love each other?'

'I don't know.' I dropped the jumper into the case. 'I think... Look, Pascal, maybe you'll hate me for saying this but I think that right now, even though I do love you, my course is the most important thing in my life. I mean...' I bit the corner of my lip. 'All I can say is this. If you were staying here, if you were going to live in Australia then I'd be rapt. I'd be over the moon. Maybe I wouldn't want us to live together but it'd be like a dream come true to have you around. But the point is, you're *not* living in Australia, you're going back to Spain and we're splitting up. It's been a holiday romance. That doesn't mean we don't take each other seriously but the holiday is over, Pascal, and I've got a really important start to make. I can't have a boyfriend tagging along.'

'I wouldn't tag,' he protested.

'But you know what I mean, don't you?'

'I guess so.'

'Then you'll change it back? Your ticket, I

mean?'

'I guess so.'

'You don't have to be so depressed about it.' I reached out and touched his cheek. 'We've done it twice so we can do it again. We can't seem to see each other without falling in love. Next time it's my turn to come to Spain. Or maybe you'll come and live in Australia when you finish your course? Who knows what's ahead of us?'

He smiled and shrugged. 'I suppose you are right.'

'Come on, Pascal,' I pulled him off the bed. 'Let's make the most of the time we've got. Let's go out. Let's have fun. Tomorrow you'll leave, and then next time...'

Pascal stood up and put his arms around me again. 'You know what, Annie?'

'What?' I grinned.

'I just love you.'